"Minka, you should know that I have a habit of coming on strong in the presence of things that appeal to me, but you don't have to be afraid of me."

She was studying the patterns painstakingly crafted into the glass constructing the spotlight several feet up. She heard his voice very close, very…soft. When she turned, he was right there looking adorable and wholly concerned that fear was the emotion she had for him.

Her expression discounted that. It was soft, bordering on amused that he could think such a thing. "Oliver that— that's crazy. You've done nothing to—"

His head dipped and he was kissing her, his tongue plundering, exploring, discovering. Minka responded with a moan that held tones of surprise and expressed need. She wasn't sure what to do with her hands—an unnecessary concern as he'd taken possession of her wrists. He held them fast as he tugged her into the unexpected kiss.

The gesture wasn't overpowering—it teased. His tongue enticed her to respond in kind yet was just as content being the lone participant in the act.

At first, Minka had been too stunned to launch right into full participation, but that eventually— deliciously—changed. His tongue continued to tantalize hers, thrusting and withdrawing during its hearty sampling of her mouth.

Dear Reader,

Treasure My Heart was a complete surprise to me. How?
Well, I was all set to write a completely different story, but
had to switch gears to spin the tale of Oliver Bauer and
Minka Gerald. I have to say it was a completely enjoyable
surprise. I did NOT expect this story to take on the life
that it did. The couple quickly became a treasure to me.
The dynamic between Oliver and Minka is one that I
hope you will feel as strongly as I did. Of course, you
know how I enjoy tossing in those dangerous little twists,
and *Treasure My Heart* will bring those to you.

So kick back with your favorite treat and spend
a little more time in California wine country with
Minka Gerald, Oliver Bauer and a few other familiar faces.

AlTonya Washington

Treasure my Heart

AlTONYA WASHINGTON

⟨H⟩HARLEQUIN® KIMANI™ ROMANCE

Recycling programs
for this product may
not exist in your area.

ISBN-13: 978-0-373-86415-7

Treasure My Heart

HARLEQUIN®

Printed in U.S.A.

™ www.Harlequin.com

AlTonya Washington has been a romance novelist for over eleven years. She's been nominated for numerous awards and has won two *RT Book Reviews* Reviewer's Choice Awards for her novels *Finding Love Again* and *His Texas Touch*. AlTonya lives in North Carolina and works as a college reference librarian. This author wears many hats, but being a mom is her favorite job.

Books by AlTonya Washington

Harlequin Kimani Romance

The Doctor's Private Visit
As Good as the First Time
Every Chance I Get
Private Melody
Pleasure After Hours
Texas Love Song
His Texas Touch
Provocative Territory
Provocative Passion
Trust In Us
Indulge Me Tonight
Embrace My Heart
Treasure My Heart

Visit the Author Profile page at Harlequin.com for more titles.

For Sara, I miss you.

Prologue

"Will, man, what—what the hell? What the hell happened?" Charles Ruggles rushed into the office to find his colleague viciously filling a leather carryall with the few personal effects he had in his office.

At the door stood two uniformed guards. They were there to ensure William Lloyd took nothing more from the Wilder Investments building than he'd brought.

"Will, man, what happened?" Charles pleaded.

"Little witch got me fired, is what," Will grumbled in a voice as sinister as the look on his attractive honey-toned face.

Charles's bewilderment continued to mount.

"Minka Gerald is a nosy little micromanager who can't let anybody outshine her in the boss's eyes." Will shoved a wad of sticky notes into the carryall.

"That doesn't sound like Minka," Charles said after expelling a low whistle.

"It's her, all right."

"Well damn, man, what happened?"

"Forget it." Will wasn't about to share what had led up to his firing, nor did he have time to come up with a believable lie. His head ached, and his thoughts were raging. He had to get out of there.

"Will—"

"Let it go, Chuck, will you?"

"This has to be some kind of mistake." Charles paced the room, rubbing his jaw. "Sim's always raving about what a good job you're doing with the foundation." He referred to the boss, Qasim Wilder. Will had been the point person for Qasim's Wilder Warriors Foundation since he'd been hired.

"Why don't I talk to him—"

"No, Chuck, please. It's cool, all right?"

"Sim's a reasonable guy, you know?"

"I appreciate the effort, Chuck, really," Will said earnestly. "Wish there were more folks like you in the world, but this is nothin' but the same ol' same ol'. I'm used to it—they get off on treating us like crap."

Charles let the comment slide, not quite sure who Will meant by *they* or *us*. "Is there *anything* I can do?" he asked.

Will smirked. "Get Congress to pass a bill ordering the country to treat war vets like humans." He shook his head, finished up his ferocious packing and slung the strap of the carryall across his shoulder. He rounded the desk.

"Thanks, Chuck." Will extended a hand. "You always treated me like somebody, and I appreciate it."

"Pleasure workin' with you, Will," Charles smiled earnestly. "You're good people."

Will left with a curt nod, and then stormed down the hallway with the guards in tow. He arrived in the executive corridor in time to see Minka Gerald, the chief admin and right hand to Qasim Wilder.

Minka approached her desk from the private corridor leading to the president's wing. Will watched her round the desk and stand there, shuffling through a stack of papers.

"Happy, Mink?" he called while punching the elevator's down button. He gave the button a second forceful stab for good measure and then looked down the hall to glare at Minka.

"I guess I should be thanking you." His smile was cold. "Sim said I'd most likely be walkin' out of this place in cuffs if you hadn't dragged your feet on getting me that signing document. Funny, I don't feel like I'm much in your debt."

Minka let the papers fall back to her desk. "You're right." She strode past her desk to face him. "You shouldn't feel in my debt. It's Qasim you betrayed, even when he gave you numerous chances to redeem yourself. You just went right on disrespecting him by stealing from a charity to help *kids*, of all people."

"Disrespect?" Will sneered, turning slightly from the elevators. "Disrespect? *I* was the one who saved *his* life, you—"

"Watch it, Lloyd" one of the guards breathed.

"Nah, Wayne, let him go on and say it," the other guard said, smiling at Minka. "No offense, Ms. G., but I've been itchin' for a chance to acquaint my fist with this fool's face."

"I'd break your hand before you even clenched that fist." Will's gaze never veered from Minka's face.

Minka refused to look away, refused to give Will Lloyd the satisfaction of knowing he'd rattled her.

Will smiled as though he knew Minka's attempt to remain unfazed had failed. He nodded. "Thanks for all you've done... *Ms. G.* Be seein' ya."

The elevator dinged. One of the guards followed Will inside. The other waited, his dark features drawn in concern.

"You okay, Minka?"

She blinked, putting a phony smile in place. "Yeah, Paul, thanks. I'm good." She gave him a wave and watched him disappear inside the elevator.

Alone, she returned to her desk and expelled a weighted breath.

Chapter 1

Saint Helena, CA

Oliver Bauer's hand hovered over the ignition switch of his Jeep. Inside him, undying male desire, curiosity and a fair amount of recklessness were waging war. All dictated that he follow the curvy sliver of chocolate who had just bounced out of his sister's home.

"Hopeless," he murmured, bowing his head to rub a few fingers through the almond-brown curls complimenting his cinnamon skin. Silently, he acknowledged that his "conquest at all costs" frame of mind would get him in over his head one day.

Oliver climbed out of the Jeep. Still, he couldn't resist another look toward the woman who was settling behind the wheel of a chocolate Benz, with personalized plates that read LUVMINK.

Oliver watched the car until it took a left down the road to the main gate at Carro Vineyards. The vineyard and world-renowned winery had been in Oliver's family for decades. Was LUVMINK there for business? Business associates were usually shown to the door, though, weren't they? The woman had left as if she was quite familiar with his sister's house.

Oliver shook his head, silently chastising his thoughts. It was too damn early in the morning for such fantasizing, and besides, he was there on business. Oliver headed toward the house, walking right in the unlocked door.

Locked doors during the day were rare around Carro Vineyards. Even in the nearby neighborhood, where many Carro employees resided, few saw the need to secure their doors. Oliver had always adored that feeling of contentment, of safety, that seemed to permeate everything in Carro. He supposed that was one reason he had never strayed too far from home.

He maintained a small house in the nearby Carro Acres neighborhood and a more fashionable condo in San Francisco.

As he walked in, Oliver was greeted with a hug and kiss from head housekeeper Charlotte Sweeny.

"Have you had breakfast?" Charlotte asked once she'd stepped back from the hug.

"I was gonna grab something later." Oliver knew the explanation wouldn't sit well.

Charlotte grimaced. "*Something*, huh?" She reached up to pat Oliver's cheek in a gesture that danced a very fine line between affectionate and reproving.

Oliver's guileless grin accentuated his very handsome face.

"You need to take better care of yourself." She gave his arm a halfhearted shove.

"That's what I have you for." Oliver dropped another kiss on her cheeck.

Charlotte only shook her head. "Don't go missing on me." She turned. "I'm going to get you some breakfast. Your sister's in the library," she called.

Oliver watched the woman walk off and sighed. Silently, he tried to talk himself out of what he was about to do. "Charlotte?" *Hopeless.* "Um, I don't want to disturb Vecs if she's busy," he said. "I saw someone leaving when I was pulling up."

Charlotte thought for a moment and then her expression cleared. "Are you talking about Minka?"

"Minka." Oliver hoped that his expression was cool enough to mask the heat that filtered through his voice when he spoke the woman's unusual name. "She a new friend?" He couldn't recall her from his sister's small, practically nonexistent list of female acquaintances.

"I'd like to think so." If Charlotte was curious about Oliver's interest in the woman, she didn't let on. "I'm hoping she'll be a more frequent visitor. Seems she and Vectra are becoming pretty close. I guess we have Qasim to thank for that."

"Sim?" Oliver thought of the respected financier who was also an old friend. Qasim Wilder was his sister's new, and from the looks of it, permanent love.

Charlotte was nodding. "Ms. Gerald is Qasim's right hand at Wilder, you know?"

Minka Gerald. Oliver repeated the name silently and may have put it on loop had Charlotte not swatted his arm.

"Stop stalling. I'll be right back with breakfast,

and you better not leave before I put something in that tummy of yours!" Charlotte hurried down the corridor.

"Yes, ma'am." Oliver's grin renewed, and he savored the woman's knack for making him feel like he was eight years old again. An instant later, he set off to find his sister.

Vectra Bauer waved for her brother to enter when she saw him peek into the library. She was on the phone. The cradle of a powder-blue cordless was tucked in the crook of her neck as she shuffled through folders on a high worktable.

"I have them right here," she said into the phone. "Sorry I haven't had a chance to go through them yet... Mmm-hmm...Okay, that sounds good."

Oliver strode over to the table, relieving his little sister of the file she held. He thumbed through the folder. Thick, sleek brows drew close when he saw material he recognized.

"If you give me another few hours to review it all, I should have more input by this evening," Vectra was saying. "I'm sure we can give you what you want, but I'd like to look over the photos before we fully commit... Right...Right...Okay, then. Thanks, Austin, we'll talk tonight."

"What's up?" Oliver waved the file once Vectra put the phone down.

Vectra eased a tuft of her clipped hair behind an ear and smiled. "The photographers you hired are about to have a gallery showing. Austin Sharpe wants photos of the new space you acquired for him to be featured at an event he wants to hold at Gallery V-Miami." She referenced one of two art galleries she owned.

"And he wants *that* featured in your gallery?" he asked playfully.

Vectra gave a light shrug beneath the auburn robe she wore over PJs of the same color. "He says he wants to think outside the box. He's pulling out every stop to wow his clients."

Oliver was once again browsing through the file of glossy eight-by-ten shots. The photographers had been hired by his staff to capture Sharpe's new office park in South Beach, Miami.

"Sim involved in this?" he asked.

Vectra's expression softened.

Oliver let out a playful groan when he saw Vectra's dreamy expression.

She elbowed past him, away from the worktable. "I guess he'll be involved since Austin's a client."

"That why his assistant was here?"

"Yeah, she—" Vectra turned, sending Oliver a measuring look. "How'd you know that?"

"Saw her leaving." Oliver tossed the Sharpe file to the table and leaned back against it.

"You've met her?"

"Nope. Never saw her before today."

"How'd you know it was her?" Vectra's curiosity amplified.

Oliver suddenly seemed interested in the cuffs of the navy shirt peeking from his beige blazer. "I asked," he said.

"Asked who?"

His smile was all cunning, with not a shred of guilt. "Charlotte."

"Olive," Vectra said firmly. "No, Oliver."

"I take it you've known her for a while."

"Quite a while."

"And you never introduced me."

"Jeez, Olive." Vectra rolled her eyes and continued toward the sofa. "It's not like I've been hiding her. She works for Qasim, and you get together with him often."

"We rarely get together in each other's offices."

"Too bad, since that's where she usually is." Vectra shrugged and claimed a spot on the sofa with an airy grace.

"Why haven't you introduced me?" He pinned her with his stare.

Her gaze reflected more sternness. "Do you really need me to answer that?"

Sudden regret tinged his eyes. His sister had few female friends. Few? "None" was perhaps a more apt estimation. Vectra definitely had what it took to garner swarms of friends, but she never had actually set out to make any. While she had passing acquaintances, he knew she longed for friendship that had more meaning. So many potential friendships had lost their luster when it became quite clear that those women had used the possibility of *her* friendship as a way to obtain *his*.

"Is that why you didn't introduce me? Afraid I'd steal away another potential friend?"

"Oh." Vectra gave a wave and appeared amused. "I don't think I'll have to worry about that with Minka. She's got a standing rule against dating anyone she knows through business."

"And yet you've known her all this time and never mentioned her to me." He intentionally overlooked the point she was trying to make.

Vectra let her head fall back against the sofa.

"Olive…" She shook her head against the cushions and then straightened. "Leave it alone, why don't you?"

Oliver left the worktable and went for the breakfast cart that had been brought in for Vectra earlier. He opted for a glass of OJ instead of his preferred black, unsweetened coffee.

"Is she married?" he asked.

"No." Vectra sighed, intent on surveying the monogram of her initials etched into the oversized cuff of her robe.

Oliver sipped the juice and debated the reply. "Seeing someone?" he tried.

"Not that I'm aware of, and just so we can wrap up this part of the conversation, the biggest reason for not introducing you to her is because I just value your life a little too much."

Oliver hesitated before taking another sip of the juice. "Value my life?" He laughed.

Vectra appeared thoroughly unamused. "Qasim will kill you if you do Minka wrong in any way, and I'd probably help him." She leaned forward, crossing her wrists over her knees. "Minka's not the type you just call up when you need your ego…and other things… stroked. She deserves more than a guy who doesn't believe in 'sleeping over.' She deserves to be treasured and to be the only one. You've made it clear that you're not looking for that. Has that changed?" She waited for his response, the expression on her lovely cinnamon-toned face proving she already knew the answer.

Oliver set aside the juice glass. "No." He gave a quick shake of his head. "That hasn't changed."

Vectra nodded as though she were satisfied. She scooted closer to the coffee table, where folders lay marked with the Carro Vineyards logo. "Now, if we're done discussing the sad state of your love life, I've got some questions about these documents you need my proxy for."

Oliver obliged, joining his sister on the sofa. "For the record, my love life is not sad. I laugh often," he grumbled.

Vectra selected the folder she was most interested in. "There's a difference between laughing because something's funny and laughing because you're happy."

Grimacing, Oliver relieved her of the folder. "Anyone ever tell you you've got a weird philosophical outlook? Sunny too."

"I'm not trying to put you down, Olive." Vectra smiled off the teasing criticism and squeezed his arm. "You'll understand once you're ready to."

But what if I'm never ready to?

Petaluma, CA

Located in Sonoma County, Petaluma was a picturesque historic town about an hour's drive from San Francisco. It boasted an impressive reputation as a shooting locale for several major Hollywood films.

The town was also well-known for its numerous poultry farms. It was how Minka Gerald's grandfather Bryant Gerald had earned his first million in a time when such success was virtually unheard of, especially for an African-American man.

Bryant's business savvy motivated him to not only experiment with cutting-edge methods and techniques to streamline his farm, but also to branch out into other lucrative areas of industry. Those areas had taken him to billionaire status long before his passing seven years prior.

Minka parked at the top of a brick horseshoe drive, and frowned amusedly as she stepped out. "Well, hey!" she said to the portly mocha-skinned gentleman who strode down the five semicircular steps.

"Gram Z. said you were leaving on vacation," Minka said as she drew close for a hug.

Claudio Moritz put a kiss to both of Minka's cheeks. "I decided to take a later flight when Zena told me you were coming up for a visit," he explained.

"How is she?" Minka sighed, looking toward the palatial Georgian home set in an expansive estate. She smiled when Claudio grunted a laugh.

"Kickin' ass and not bothering to take names, because she doesn't care whose ass she kicks," he said.

"Hold on now." Minka wagged a finger at the seventysomething Haitian. "You're supposed to be handling things so she won't have to kick any asses."

"Are we talkin' about the same woman?" Claudio's expression was one of mock surprise. "About yea high, moves around this place like hell on wheels and'll curse you out like a sailor if you even hint that she needs to slow down? *That* woman?"

Minka's laughter echoed in the crisp air. "You *are* her first cousin, remember?"

"Lovely." Claudio fixed Minka with a teasing look of woe. "If your own granddad couldn't get that woman to slow down, how in Hades do you expect me to?"

More laughter soared between the two. Claudio was the first to sober.

"She still misses him." He looked toward the house.

Minka nodded, knowing as much. "I guess one never gets over their true love."

"Especially when it's a first love," Claudio added with a decisive nod.

Minka put a refreshing smile in place. "Can you tell me what she wants?"

"No idea." Claudio put on a phony display of innocence when he shrugged. "What else could it be when grandmother and granddaughter spend time together, except the sweetest things?"

"Mmm-hmm, *sweet* things like when I'll make her a *great*-grandmother." Minka sighed, her tone only playfully agitated.

Claudio added a chuckle as he nodded. "Will it make you feel better to know there will be talk of business too?"

Minka read Claudio's caginess and knew that he'd tell her nothing of further use. "Thanks for the info," she said and pulled him in for another hug before they parted ways.

The stateliness of Zena Gerald's home was equally evident on the interior. Rooms were posh, yet comfortably designed.

The house, with its open spaces and picture windows that revealed views of rolling greens, sky-blue hues and colorful floral splashes, gave one the impression that they were standing in the middle of a breathtaking watercolor painting.

"Babylove!"

Minka turned into the sound of her grandmother's melodic voice and rushed into the woman's embrace. Though she had just seen Zena a couple of weeks earlier, it always felt like months between the visits. Minka adored spending time with the energetic, outspoken woman.

"Thank you for being prompt." Zena Moritz Gerald cupped her granddaughter's face and gave a squeeze.

"I just saw you a couple of weeks ago." Minka patted her grandmother's hands where they lay on her face. "Did this just come up?"

"It's a talk we've needed to have for quite a while." Zena planted a soft kiss on Minka's mouth and then hugged her. "We shouldn't postpone it any longer."

"Gram Z...." Gently, Minka took hold of the woman's arm when she would've walked away. "Is everything okay?" Her dark eyes were assessing her grandmother's slender figure.

"Oh!" Zena rolled her eyes. "It's nothing like that. I feel very fine. Although..." She intentionally let the word hang while her expressive eyes scanned the high ceiling of the foyer. "I do feel like I'm wasting away roaming around this house and that god-awful office building of your grandfather's."

"That building is a work of art." Minka took her grandmother by the arm and led her from the foyer.

"Work of art or not, it's hard to enjoy it if you don't want to be there."

"Which I'm guessing is what brings us to the purpose of this visit?" Minka continued to prompt.

"Your father was slated to be the one to take over, being our only son and only child," Zena explained as they walked down a short corridor leading to a sun-drenched parlor. "But...you know how that's turning out..."

Silence settled as grandmother and granddaughter covered the distance to the parlor. Minka walked ahead of Zena as they entered the room, which opened on to a split-level wraparound terrace, part of which over-looked a pool below.

"Your parents said nothing about coming back to the States when I spoke to them last week," Zena said while taking time to water-spritz the arrangement of lilies and yellow tulips on the glass stand just inside the door.

Minka's parents, Brice and Leslie Gerald, had lived in France for the past four years. Minka knew that Zena hoped they'd return, but Minka could hear the lightness, the happiness in her parents' voices whenever she spoke to them. Returning to the States was definitely not on their agendas at the moment.

"They're not coming back," Zena confirmed. "Not to work anyway, which means the job is yours, my love." She spread her hands, as if offering Minka a prize.

Minka's eyes widened. "Gram Z….you said…you said you'd never do that to me no matter how much I wanted it. It was one of the reasons I went to work for Sim."

"You're right, honey, I did." Zena began to walk through the parlor, water-spritzing the various arrangements of flowers brightening the space. "I said that because I wanted you to get out there and get more experience. You going to work for Qasim was a godsend."

Minka could only frown. She wasn't sure what question to ask next.

"Being over at Wilder, where no one knew your background, your family, your…money, I'd hoped you'd gain more than just a reputation as Qasim's efficient, take-no-prisoners assistant."

"Ah, jeez…" Minka closed her eyes. "Gram Z.—"

"I wanted you to come out of there with a husband, or at the very least some kind of meaningful relationship."

"Gram, I wouldn't have been any good at my job had I gone there looking for love."

Zena gave in to a bit of soft laughter while spraying a vibrant vine that rippled all the way to the hardwood floor. "Such dedication to business." Her dark eyes sparkled with both humor and regret. "You're as ambitious as your granddad and your father," she sighed, turning to Minka. "But at least your father had enough of *my* genes to get out of it and focus on what was most important. I wish *you* had gained those particular genes."

"Me?" Minka straightened in her chair. "Why?"

"Being ambitious and business obsessed is expected of men. It doesn't keep them from being drawn to women and companionship, but it tends to have the opposite effect on women." She set aside the water bottle and began to stroll the room again.

"Women tend to shy away from husbands and families in pursuit of our goals," Zena added.

Minka shook her head. "That's not true, Gram."

"It is in your case, though, isn't it?"

Minka stood. "So you called me here to discuss my nonexistent love life." *Again*, she tacked on silently.

"No." Zena's calm was unshakeable. "I asked you here to offer you the keys to the kingdom, so to speak. Bryant G Industries is yours, my love."

"Gram." Minka joined the woman on the other side of the room. "Be serious with me now. Are you okay, really?"

Zena laughed, the sound as bright and airy as the sunny flower-dotted room around her. "Babylove, I promise you I'm fine. I'm not about to kick the bucket, but there *are* things I'd like to do before the bucket is kicked." She tugged at the cream-and-mocha ties around Minka's figure-flattering dress and fixed her granddaughter with a stern look.

"Your grandfather always wanted a family presence in the building, *and* he wanted it to be family he trusted. You've been groomed for this your entire life." Zena sniffed disdainfully. "Perhaps we groomed you too well for business when we should've spent time on home-ec."

"So when do I start?" Minka asked after shaking her head over the "home ec" remark.

"Oh, there's plenty of time, but it's going to require lots of big changes on your part, so you should be ready."

"Yeah…" Some of Minka's budding excitement began to wane as thoughts of leaving her job at Wilder took shape.

"You'll be acquainting yourself with BGI business associates that you may not know," Zena said, "and even though others will be on hand to handle the day-to-day management of those clients, meeting you in person will go a long way to enhance those relationships. I'll keep you posted on those dates."

Minka only nodded. She didn't want to reveal too much of her excitement.

Of course, Zena saw it clearly enough. "Your grandfather wanted family to take over, but I *will* find someone else to put in this space, child, if that's what I have to do. My plan is to announce my successor at the stockholders' meeting. I want you to use the time between now and then to figure out if this is really the life you want."

"I'm not a hermit, Gram."

"No, but my guess is that when you take an interest in a man, it's not because you see him as a potential life partner."

"Gee, thanks!"

Zena shrugged off her granddaughter's outrage. "You know what I mean. This is one woman speaking to another now, Mi-Mi."

Minka stiffened her stance and nodded. "A woman doesn't have the same freedoms in business that a man does, Gram. I'm sure things weren't easy for you when word got out that you were dating your boss."

"Ha! Especially during *those* times." Zena laughed, her dark eyes glimmering in remembrance.

"The gossip spread all the way to my parents," Zena recalled, "through their well-meaning church members, of course." She let out a purely girlish giggle and sighed. "At least they got it right. Bryant and I were quite the scandal. I'm sure we christened every floor of that gorgeous office building of his."

Minka felt her cheeks heat even as laughter tickled her throat.

"Sorry, love." Zena winked. "Your ears are still a little too young to hear about such romps." She patted Minka's cheeks and took a seat on the cushioned window seat that lined the length of the room.

"Things between your grandfather and I weren't just physical, Mi-Mi. Bryant was just as interested in the way my mind worked when it came to business. Don't close yourself off to a man because you're afraid of what the world may think."

Minka stood, quietly absorbing the advice.

"You'll be surprised how the world fades into the background when a man you'd give anything to be with steps into the picture. And you'll be just as surprised by what's going to be demanded of you once you sit in the main chair. You'll do well to have a man who not only understands what that responsibility means, but who also reminds you that responsibility isn't *all* your world consists of."

Zena sighed, satisfied that she'd delivered enough advice. "Just something to think about. Come on, Baby-love. We'll have tea on the terrace," she said as she walked out of the parlor.

Minka rushed though the door of her dinner event for the Sharpe Organization and was relieved to see that the event had yet to begin.

The open bar was already being well used. Apparently the organization's leader, Austin Sharpe, wanted his attendees nice and pliable before the meeting commenced.

Thoroughly pliable, if the level of intoxication of a few of the attendees was any indication. The room had been decorated with Southwestern flair, and the menu reflected the theme. She barely had time to get a drink of her own before she was cornered by one of her colleagues.

Charles Ruggles began slurring his opinions to her about why they should partner up over the course of the next several weeks to ensure that the Sharpe project went off without a hitch.

"Jus' makes sense for us to join force—*forces* to ensure it all goes smooth…"

Minka stifled a laugh over Charles's crooning of the last word. "Maybe we should hold off on setting any private meetings until we know more about what Sharpe has in store for us, don't you think?"

Charles twisted his mouth. "Nope." He smacked the word after a moment's consideration.

"Why don't we discuss it after the meeting?" She moved to excuse herself from where he'd huddled her against a wall.

Charles wasn't quite done making his pitch. "You know this'll involve us at some point…" He barred her escape with a hand planted against the wall. His other hand still clutched a glass carrying traces of vodka tonic. "You'll enjoy how well we'll work together—"

"Ms. Gerald? Could I have a minute?"

Minka looked over Charles's head to the much taller man behind him, and her agitation instantly softened. Charles was still too absorbed in his drunken wooing to notice the interruption.

Minka's gaze fixed on the stranger with the steady light brown eyes. She nodded just slightly to accept the man's request, and looked on in wonder as he eased Charles aside and gently laid claim to her arm.

Chapter 2

"Thank you." Minka smiled as the stranger led her through the crowded dining area to another unoccupied corner of the room.

"There was no need for a rescue. He's harmless," she said, her heart flipping when she looked up at her escort.

Wait a minute...flipped? The idea gave Minka pause, but yes, her heart had definitely performed some sort of acrobatic feat when the man's gaze had met hers. She looked on as a curious smile curved his wide, carefully crafted mouth.

"You think I did that for you?" Unhurried, he released her arm. "I was just trying to help the guy. He really shouldn't go into a meeting with a black eye. It's not a good look."

Minka laughed, her head falling back and her eyes closing. She missed seeing the stranger's curious smile evolve into a provocative grin as he appraised her lovely dark face.

"I'll have to make sure Charles comes over later to thank you for saving his face from your fist," Minka said once she'd sobered from her laughter.

"Best to hold off on bringing him near me till after the meeting, or else he's liable to get that black eye, after all." The stranger smiled, then extended his hand. "Oliver Bauer."

Minka settled her hand into his. "Minka Gerald," she said.

"I know who you are."

Minka waited for those extraordinary eyes of his to take a trail downward, just like they always did when men first met her. Besides, the cut of her black wrap dress offered quite the irresistible view.

Oliver Bauer's gaze took no such journey, however. Minka didn't know if she felt more disappointment or offense over the slight. She blinked again, confusion pooling her eyes.

"Bauer? You're related to Vectra." It wasn't a question. Her new friend and this man shared the most entrancing eye color—a light walnut-brown shade. In Oliver Bauer's eyes, though, there lurked a playful, almost rakish look.

"She's my sister," Oliver confirmed.

Minka frowned. "I thought she said you were older?"

"Well, I am." He feigned offense that she didn't think he was. "By eighteen months, thank you very much."

"Your parents didn't waste any time, did they?"

Oliver shrugged. "My folks never wasted time when it came to sex."

Minka surrendered to more laughter. "I'm sorry."

She gave a quick shake of her head and cleared her throat. "You said there was something you needed to talk to me about?"

Broad shoulders lifted beneath an olive-brown suit coat. "Not really." His tempting mouth curved into a crooked smile. "I just didn't much care for *him* talking to you, is all." He inclined his head in the general direction of Charles Ruggles. His eyes never left Minka's face. "Ms. Gerald." He nodded once slightly, then made his retreat.

"So you've all heard the proposal," Austin Sharpe said once his guests had settled around the meeting table. "Your minds are relaxed by drink and unoccupied by hunger." Austin grinned while his audience laughed. "Do I have any questions?"

All around the table were representatives from the companies Austin had tapped to play a role in his bold venture.

"Yes, sir?" Austin sent an encouraging smile across the square table toward the man who had raised a hand.

"Thank you, sir. I'm Ed Summeral—Wilder, VP Marketing," the freckle-faced redhead said.

Austin's welcoming smile remained. "Go on, Ed."

"Thank you, sir, uh." Ed moved to allow a server to top off the coffee Charles Ruggles had been drinking since the onset of the meeting.

"Sir, what part will Wilder, specifically the marketing team, have to play in this venture?"

"Good question, Ed." Austin ticked an index finger in the VP's direction. "This will be the marketing team's turn to shine and get some credit for all that back-breaking work your boss loads on you."

Everyone laughed at Qasim Wilder, who sat next to Vectra.

"My clients know I trust Wilder with my money, which means I trust Wilder with *their* money too," Austin continued. "This is your chance to show them why. The same goes for all the departments represented here tonight. It'll be exciting to see how you toot your horns."

More laughter followed as hands rose more freely following the opening question. Minka took notes on the queries from Wilder staff. Chances were high that she'd have to help the various departments at Wilder "toot their horns."

Absently, she toyed with a loose jaw-length curl. She glanced away from the pad and locked in on Oliver Bauer's bright, potent gaze fixed on her. The heat of self-awareness coursed through her, and Minka cast a subtle glance toward Qasim and Vectra.

The room and the square table were relatively large, but anyone paying close enough attention would be able to pinpoint the object of Oliver's stare. Thankfully, Minka thought, no one else seemed to notice.

She looked down at her pad again and only made a pretense at note taking. Another hand rose, this one belonging to Rita Waymore, the floor manager for Gallery V in San Francisco.

"Mr. Sharpe, you've stated that Wilder handles your money, and we all know Bauer Development acquires your land and builds your executive parks, but what part will our gallery serve?"

Austin nodded approvingly and smiled. "The part your gallery will serve is the one I'm most excited about, because it's an unprecedented one. The work done by Oliver and his team at Bauer D is staggering. We've all seen it and can attest to that, I'm sure?"

The room livened with sudden applause and cheer. Only then did Minka risk looking over at Oliver. Her heart performed another of its acrobatic flips when she saw that he was still staring her way. He had no qualms about allowing a few seconds to pass before he acknowledged the applause with a smile and wave.

"I'd like for Gallery V to showcase that genius," Austin Sharpe said. "My hope is that the skills that have earned Gallery V a reputation as one of the most cutting-edge art galleries on the East and West coasts will create a dazzling showcase of the new Sharpe Executive Business Park in South Beach, Miami." Austin waved with a flourish.

"Gallery V's creator, Vectra Bauer, assures me that such a request is child's play for her dynamic staff."

Another round of enthusiastic applause erupted.

"Well, this concludes my presentation, folks." Austin beamed as he surveyed the group. "We'll all be meeting many more times over the course of the next several weeks."

"I urge you all to remain a little longer and get to know one another. We're all going to be spending lots of time together," he added before giving a final salute and reclaiming his seat.

Conversation colored the room at once. Some remained chatting at the table, while others collected at the elaborate hot-beverage-and-dessert buffet that had been set up.

Minka was drawn aside by Wilder's financial consultants. She focused on the conversation and took notes on the group's preliminary ideas for wowing Sharpe's Miami clients.

Much of the staff at Wilder questioned Minka's decision to remain Qasim's assistant when she so clearly had a talent in other areas. Alas, Minka was happiest helping her boss and friend, and more important, it kept her privileged background off the radar.

The consultant team made plans for a lunch meeting the following afternoon. Once they parted ways, Minka decided it'd be in her best interest to get lost while she could. It had been a long day, what with the drive and visit with her grandmother in Petaluma as well as the drive back to San Francisco in time for the Sharpe meeting.

She was wiped and made quick work of packing her tablet, pens and notepads in her tan portfolio tote. Despite her determination to make an exit, she paused and gave in to one last look at Oliver.

He was tall, but height seemed to run in their family. He had the kind of lean, muscular frame that Minka was sure would make him a formidable opponent on a basketball court. Dressed as he was in a tailored three-piece, she couldn't help but appreciate the breadth of his frame. Even at rest, he seemed on alert somehow, as if he were ready to act in an instant if necessary.

He hadn't bothered to get up and mingle, she'd observed. She supposed there was no need when a number of the meeting's attendants made a point of stopping by his place at the table to hold brief conversations. Minka could tell that a great deal of the men were business as well as personal acquaintances.

She wasn't sure what to make of the women. A number of them had stopped by to chat or…simply be seen with him. Who could blame them? Cinnamon-skinned with that luxurious crop of almond-brown curls…he was gorgeous. The hypnotic gaze was such an undeniable draw, especially when paired with a perfectly crafted nose, a generous, alluring mouth, a wide forehead and a faint cleft in his chin.

Minka closed her eyes and inhaled. Evidently, she'd observed him more closely than she'd realized during their earlier encounter. *And you should go home before you do something really stupid, Mink.*

Minka dug out her car keys and snapped the tote bag shut. She turned and smiled, genuinely happy to see Qasim and Vectra approaching.

"Quite the cast of characters." Minka turned an assessing gaze toward the mingling crowd. "It'll be great to see it all come together."

"Yeah, it'll be almost a shame to miss it." Qasim Wilder looked to the woman at his side. He appraised Vectra with one meaningful sweep of his ebony gaze along her body. "Almost," he added.

Minka smiled curiously while looking between the two. "Am I missing something?"

"No," Qasim sighed the word and gave Vectra another look. "But we might. We're thinking about getting lost for a while. So I want you to put together a team for this Miami trip." Qasim eased a hand into one black trouser pocket and studied the room.

"Austin's not looking to get things started down there for another week or so…" He looked back to Minka with an encouraging smile. "I'll support whomever you tap to send."

"Sim." Minka rolled her eyes. "You know me well

enough to know I can't pick a team for something that important unless one of us goes along too."

Qasim's very dark, very gorgeous face was a study in disapproval. "You deserve to get away more than anybody. We've got a good group, so give 'em some credit."

"If you don't mind me saying, Minka," Vectra chimed in, "from what I've heard, your boss is a real slave driver. You should take the time while he's offering."

Minka laughed. "Well, it *is* Miami. I promise you guys I'll take time to enjoy it."

"Well, if you change your mind—"

"I won't." Minka shook her head to Qasim's worry. "And Gram Z. already ordered me to take some time too."

Qasim's curiosity was piqued. "How's she doin'?" he asked.

"Good." Minka nodded with a quick smile. "She's ready to give up her crown."

Qasim's curiosity melted into understanding. "Do we need to talk?"

"Yeah." Minka's nod was a bit more somber then. "I'll see you tomorrow?" She smiled when he reciprocated her nod and then looked to Vectra and pulled her into a hug. "Have a good night."

"You too, hon." Vectra's light eyes followed Minka as she made her way out of the room, shaking hands and holding quick chats with colleagues. "What was that about?" she asked, turning back to Qasim.

"Ever heard of Bryant Gerald?"

Vectra frowned. "Gerald Industries? Bryant Gerald, the billionaire?" she blurted. "He…?" Her expression cleared. "Minka?"

Qasim inclined his head a fraction. "He was her grandfather."

Vectra's confusion mounted. "But why's she working for you?"

"Thanks."

Vectra responded with a playful eye roll and shoved Qasim's arm.

He flashed her a killer smile. "The Geralds are clients," he explained. "Minka wanted to make it on her own—she wanted a position that would keep her under the radar, but still into everything. Her grandmother approved when I offered, but Minka would've accepted anyway."

"Hmph, sounds like her." Vectra smiled. "What'd she mean about her grandmother being ready to give up her crown?"

Qasim rubbed his jaw, some of the easiness of his expression receding to a more distressed look. "Sounds like Zena Gerald wants her granddaughter back."

"Had enough already?"

Minka stopped in the restaurant vestibule when his voice reached her ears. "It's been a long day." She found Oliver Bauer closing the distance between them. "And it's going to be an even longer night," she said.

Oliver made a face. "Surely you get to take *one* day off? Sim won't object to that, will he?"

"No." She smiled. "But I would."

"Ah." He appeared satisfied. "It's good to know Qasim at least *tries* to get you to take a break."

"He tries. Rarely succeeds."

"Interesting." He leaned against a wall in the vestibule. "You always get what you want?" He seemed very interested in the possibility.

Minka sighed, scanning the restaurant entrance as though she were taking time to seriously consider his query. "I think that only happens when it's something I want bad enough. No sense fighting for it if it's something you're just going to lose interest in, don't you think?"

"Hold on." He brought two fingers to his brow and tapped them there. "I need time to think about that. Seems I've fought for a lot of things I've lost interest in." He lowered his fingers, shrugged. "Sort of a blow to realize I've wasted a lot of time."

"Consider it proof that you're maturing."

Oliver winced. "My sister'll be happy to hear that."

Minka felt herself staring, adoring... With effort she tugged her gaze from his exceptional face. "I really need to get home—"

"Are you going out to Miami?"

Her movements settled. "I'm sure I will be."

"More work."

"It's Miami," she rebutted with a smile.

He grinned. "Right. So I'll see you there."

"You're going?"

"It's Miami."

She laughed softly. "Good night, Mr. Bauer."

"My dad's the only one who enjoys that Mr. Bauer stuff. My friends call me Oliver." He gave a quick tilt of his head.

"Friends?" Her frown was teasing. "Have I reached that status already?"

"You think you're unworthy?"

"I don't know you. You don't know me."

"Right." He nodded, bumping his fist to his jaw. "I see your point. Guess that means we're going to have to change that." He held the door for her. "Good night, Ms. Gerald."

Chapter 3

Minka tuned in to her phone's ringing and reached for it, hoping to catch the call before it went to voice mail.

"This is Minka." She was preoccupied with folders on her desk and didn't notice the lack of response on the other end of the line until a few seconds had passed. "Hello?" She shook her head and hung up, figuring she'd missed the call through her daydreaming.

Smirking, she silently noted that it wasn't even midmorning—*way* too early for daydreaming. How could she resist, though? If Oliver Bauer wasn't prime daydream material, she didn't know what was.

The night before, she'd chatted with her female colleagues at the meeting, and it was clear they all knew Oliver. It went without saying that he had a successful personal life, but there was still the question of *how* successful. She hadn't seen a ring, but knew that meant nothing. Men often went without their bands.

But she couldn't allow musings of Oliver Bauer to disrupt her workday. Things were going to be hectic enough without her being preoccupied by the sensuality that lurked in the man's exquisite eyes. She looked at the phone still in her hand, and with a tired smile, she tossed it back across her desk.

"Hey, hey, what are you doing here so early?!"

Minka saw Qasim and blurted a surprised laugh. "Where'd you come from?"

"The…elevator?" Qasim looked ready to laugh as well. "Didn't you hear the bell?"

Grimacing, Minka made a play at shuffling through the folders littering her desk. "It's been a long morning."

"Long morning, huh?" Sim slowed his steps the closer he drew to the desk. "My offer for time off still stands, you know? You could've at least slept in today."

"No…I arranged a few early meetings to follow up from the Sharpe thing last night."

"Oh, yeah…" Sim began to pat his trouser pockets.

Minka watched curiously as her boss fished out his key ring. He pulled off a long silver key and handed it to her. Accepting it, she frowned expectantly.

"It's from Vectra." He smiled. "She has a place in Miami near the gallery. She wants you to stay and enjoy it while you're there."

"That's sweet. Very sweet, but I—I can't let her do that—it's too much."

"Ah, take it." Qasim waved off her attempt to return the key. "Vectra doesn't think it's much at all. She thinks you've probably got some palace on the beach."

"What?" Minka frowned. "Why would she think that?"

Qasim shrugged, returning the key ring to his pocket.

"The heiresses to billion-dollar fortunes usually have such things, don't they?"

"Oh, no." Minka closed her eyes as if pained. "You told her?"

"I'm surprised she didn't figure it out sooner. It surprises me that a lot of people haven't figured it out already. Guess that's about to change, huh?"

"Sim…"

"Don't worry. I told her how you feel about folks knowing. She promised to keep it quiet. At least until you claim the big chair."

Minka folded her arms over her short-waist walnut brown blazer. "I haven't accepted yet."

"But you will." Straightening to his full height, Qasim waved a hand toward the corridor leading to his office. "Shall we talk now or later?"

Needing to work off a sudden case of nervous energy, Minka headed to Qasim's bar the moment she entered his office.

"She says she's got things she wants to do before she kicks the bucket, so it's time for me to do my duty, blah, blah, blah…"

Qasim grinned while getting settled at his desk. "I always said Miss Zena is a woman who knows how to live. Wish the same could be said for her granddaughter."

"Sim." Minka's head fell forward as she shook it. "Don't start. Gram wouldn't let up about me doing that very thing. She wants me to take time off and think about the job first before I accept."

"Are you sure?"

"I am about the business." Minka set coffee to brew.

"It's about more than that, though. Gram doesn't want me focusing so much on the business that I don't give any time to what she considers the most important things in life, namely having a husband and family."

"Ah…" Qasim's dark eyes narrowed as though he'd decided no further clarification was needed.

Minka shrugged and began looking for mugs. "That's why I want to go to Miami. Of course there's business to handle, but it *is* Miami. Hopefully Gram'll appreciate the effort I'm making to have fun."

"And also to keep her from worrying?" Sim guessed.

"Bit of both." Minka set silverware next to the mugs filled with steaming French roast. "I just don't think the marriage game is for me." She laughed at Qasim's look of playful outrage.

"This from the woman who gave me continuous grief over not going after Vectra in a way she approved."

"It's not the same, Sim."

"Oh?"

"I'm from a family of billionaires, Sim. A *heiress*. That's a whole different set of assumptions, Sim. A whole different kind of drama than a man would have."

"You're worried about not being able to find a man to love you for who you are." Qasim added an understanding nod. "You've thought a lot about this."

She gave a wan smile. "Sometimes it's hard not to. *But*, trips to Miami definitely make it easier."

"Good outlook." Sim's expression remained sober. "Talk to me if you need to, okay? And not just to give me your two weeks' notice either, all right?"

"I'd never leave you in a lurch!" Minka laughed.

"Mmm…the way I'm leaving you. Holding the bag on this Miami thing to run off for love."

Minka threw her head back to laugh robustly. "Love is the best reason to leave someone holding the bag."

"Try asking the person left holding the bag."

Minka spread her hands over the desk as though she were presenting it in a showcase. "You just did."

"I only want you to understand how serious I am about you talking to me," Qasim reiterated, following more laughter. "It's one thing to work to make the boss look good and another thing entirely when *you're* the boss. Just keep me in the loop, all right?"

Minka moved from behind the bar, nodded and met Qasim in the middle of the room for a hug.

Oliver Bauer was a man who worked hard and played harder. This lifestyle suited Oliver just fine—he had no desire to follow in his sister's footsteps anytime soon.

However, that was before he met Minka Gerald. Oliver silently called himself an idiot. He carried a sopping-wet sponge to his navy Jeep Cherokee, one of two that he owned. Waiting on deck to be washed were also two Jeep Wranglers and a black Benz G-Class SUV. The vehicles were already gleaming, but Oliver didn't see the harm in a little extra pampering. He was about to be out of town for the next few weeks, after all.

Suds and water coated the wheel and rim, but Oliver wasn't attacking the job with the same gusto he usually had for his vehicles.

Minka Gerald. She'd been an almost constant presence in his mind for days. She was a beauty who would not escape his notice, or his bed, until he was able to put his persuasive powers to the test. Yet his distinct... infatuation...was about more than that. It had to be.

After all, he knew tons of lovely women. But one who had practically hypnotized him? What the hell was that?

Oliver grunted out a laugh and gave the sponge another dunking. Idiotic indeed. He grimaced. He'd barely spent two hours in the woman's presence, and a fraction of that actually talking to her. There had certainly *not* been enough time for her to enchant him the way she had. Yet there he was, unable to get her out of his head.

Returning to the Jeep, Oliver attacked the job, scrubbing as if the act would set his thoughts to rights. It was some time before he faintly realized his name was being called. He quickly angled his tall frame out from under the vehicle when he recognized his father's voice.

"Mine could stand a good wash, since it looks like you're open for business." Oscar Bauer laughed when he saw his only son stand up next to the soapy SUV.

Grinning easily, Oliver tossed aside the sponge. "Just giving them a last wash before I hit the road to Miami."

"Yeah, I heard about the big meeting with Austin." Oscar nodded. "Sounds like you've got things well in hand on our end."

"Yeah, we'll see." Oliver wiped his hands on the seat of the faded denim shorts that hung low on his lean hips. "Austin's looking to pull in all kinds of new elements into this job." He rounded the back of the vehicle where his father stood.

"Sounds interesting," Oscar noted, his handsome caramel-toned face alight with curiosity.

"Yeah, interesting." Oliver shared a skeptical grin. "He wants to display the photographs of the new offices at Vecs's Miami gallery in the hopes of wooing new clients."

"That boy." Oscar chuckled. "He was always an out-of-the-box thinker."

"That hasn't changed." Oliver rubbed his jaw while regarding his father more closely. "Everything okay, Pop?"

Stepping closer, Oscar clapped a hand to Oliver's arm. "You know I'm proud of the work you're doing, Oli. The way you've stepped into my place and assumed control, just the way a president should."

Oliver gave his father a mockingly firm look. "Why do I feel like those words are about to be followed up by a huge *but*?"

Oscar squeezed his son's arm again. "I only wanted you to know that I have *no* issues whatsoever with the way you've taken over the business. I could retire today, content in the knowledge that my life's work will be well cared for."

"I'm still hearin' that *but*, Dad…" Oliver lost some of his playfulness.

"There's no *but*, kid. Not the kind you're expecting. I just don't want to offend you." Oscar managed a slight chuckle.

Doubt merging with concern, Oliver went to pull down the tailgate to one of the Cherokees. He patted the area, urging his father to sit. "Talk to me, Dad. What's up? Really?"

Oscar leaned against the edge of the lowered tailgate, but didn't sit. "Looks like we're going to have to partner up for an upcoming meeting."

"Partner up?" Oliver smiled curiously over the news. "Like when I was first learning the ropes, partner up?"

Oscar nodded, his easy expression showing signs of distress. "I know you don't need me looking over your shoulder anymore, but tag-teaming this thing would be a good idea for this particular client."

"Well, who is it?" Oliver folded his arms across the worn Lakers T-shirt that stretched over his broad chest.

"I'm still handling it more or less, but now with my impending retirement, it's going to be important for them to understand that a changing of the guard is needed."

"Is the guy difficult to work for or something?" Oliver asked.

The easiness returned to Oscar's expression as he shared a cunning grin with his son. "The *guy* wasn't difficult at all—he was a good friend as well as client— one I handled exclusively which is why you don't know him. But he's passed on, and his wife's the client now."

Oliver whistled, made a face. "How difficult is *she*?"

"Oh, not very difficult at all." Oscar laughed over his son's skeptical expression. "Seriously, she's just, um…demanding and determined to see that her demands are met."

"And she's demanding that you be present for this meeting?"

"Not exactly." Oscar leaned more heavily against the tailgate. "She doesn't know I'm about to tell her you'll be the one handling her land acquisition deals for the foreseeable future."

From his seat on the tailgate, Oliver swung one sneaker-shod foot back and forth. "Has she been pleased with our work so far?"

"So far, yes. Very pleased." Oscar scratched his whiskered jaw and looked out over the backyard. "She calls these meetings every couple of years just to get face time with the folks who handle her money and other interests."

"Don't worry, Dad. I'll be happy to be your wing-man." Oliver reached over to squeeze his father's shoulder. "You think the client will put up much fuss about the change?"

"Nah." Oscar waved off the concern. "She's a pistol, but a sweetheart."

"Well, she sounds lovely." Oliver moved off the tailgate. "Anymore details you'd like to share? Such as a name?"

Oscar grinned knowingly. "Not a chance. I know you, and I don't want you fixated on researching and trying to prepare yourself just yet." He shrugged. "I only wanted you to put this on your radar. We can save the rest until after your big trip. I'm sure I don't need to remind you to have fun while you're in Miami?"

Oliver's rakish grin was almost a replica of his father's. "No, sir, such a reminder is totally unnecessary."

"Ha!" Oscar fell in step with his son. "Don't even know why I bothered."

"Um…Dad?" Oliver's steps slowed. "Are you ever… concerned about the way I live? The way I live my life?"

Oscar erupted into a rich round of laughter. "Where the hell did *that* come from?"

"It's just with all the uh…all the women…" Oliver rubbed his fingers through his hair and gave the curls a tug. "Are you ever concerned that I won't have anything more? Like you did with Mom?"

Oscar eased his hands into the deep front pockets of his gray trousers and graced his son with a probing look. "What's gotten into you, Oli?"

"I don't know." Oliver shrugged, understanding that

the question sounded crazy coming from him. "Just somethin' Vecs said got me thinking…"

Oscar's rich laughter returned behind an even greater force then. "Letting that girl get in your head as usual, huh?!"

Oliver smiled, conceding. "I thought she might have a point."

Oscar curbed his laughter—some. "What'd she say, exactly?"

"Something about the difference between laughing because I'm happy and laughing because something's funny." Oliver shrugged, shook his head and commenced to rubbing at his curls again. "She said I'd understand what that meant when I was ready. I guess it's something folks in love would get."

"Hmph. I've been in love over half my life, but I'm still not quite sure I get your little sister's philosophy on that one."

The men shared a laugh, and then Oscar quieted.

"Being amused to the point of laughter is just a reaction to something at the moment," he said, walking as he theorized. "*Happiness* is a condition—a state of being—something more sustaining. Only love instills happiness like that."

A poignant gleam crept into Oliver's light eyes as he studied his father and shrugged. "See? It's something folks in love would get. Like I said."

"Is that regret I'm hearing in your voice, kid?"

"More curiosity than regret, I think." Oliver studied the ground as he spoke. "Dad when we…lost Mom… me and Vectra, we…we worried about you. It was scary to see what love and…the loss of it can do to a person, even a person as strong as you."

Something haunted crossed Oscar's face at the mention of his beloved late wife, Rose. "When I lost her, I hated the world and God for it. I wanted to shut them both out." A smile fought through the darkness of his expression.

"No matter how raw I felt, how much it hurt…it was worth it. It was worth it to know love like that." He looked at his son. "That's what I want for you and your sister."

"I'm afraid I'm a creature of habit, Dad."

Oscar fell in step with his son as they headed toward the rugged A-frame in the heavily wooded outskirts of Carro land. "You know the best way to get rid of an old habit, son?" He clapped the middle of Oliver's back. "Replace it with a new passion."

South Beach, Miami

As soon as Minka crossed the threshold of Vectra Bauer's stunning condo, she knew she wouldn't be in the mood for the meetings and events scheduled for the Sharpe account.

The condo's floor-to-ceiling windows offered sun-splashed glimpses of a large invisible pool beyond which lay the captivating brilliance of South Beach. Minka was certain that it would take her at least a week before she was ready to leave the gorgeous condo.

Scratch that, she was certain it would take her at least a week before she was ready to leave the *master bathroom.*

Rose-blush marble dominated the flooring as well as the shower and tub areas. It also ran the length of the counter space, merging into the rich dark oak finish of the cabinets at the rear of the split-level room. Golden light from electric candles outlined a recessed bay mirror from which a glass mantel protruded. The space supported a row of hand-carved brass candle holders filled with candles that highlighted the rose-blush color scheme.

The floor tiles were sparsely covered with plush area rugs of the same color. Minka decided the color had to be one of Vectra Bauer's favorites. The rugs beckoned visitors to cast off socks and sink their toes into their warmth.

Despite the room's warm spacious quality, the most show-stopping element had to be the tub. A work of art, the square rose-blush marble tub sat atop a platform made of the same oak as the cabinets.

Of course it was irresistible, so much so that Minka decided a long, bubbly soak would be first on her to-do list. She started to undress in the middle of the gorgeous bathroom, only pausing to select a bath gel from Vectra's unbelievable stock of aromatherapy products located in a cabinet beneath the tub's platform.

Ten minutes later, she was submerged in white foam and hot water. Laughter began to tickle her tummy as she relaxed for the first time in weeks.

She thought about her career so far. Going against the norm worked for her, and it had been a large factor in her decision to work outside her family's company. The life of a working girl had suited her just fine. Now, her grandmother needed her to assume her rightful place at the head of BGI.

It went without saying that she was up for the challenge. She was perceptive enough to know that Qasim hadn't given freedom or authority at Wilder because he was such a firm believer in delegating authority. But he knew her pedigree—knew she'd been business educated since she could talk. Now, she was about to see if all the preparation had paid off. As Qasim had said, it was another thing entirely to be the one sitting in the chair.

For the time being, however, she was content with lounging in a fabulously decadent tub. She fell into hypnotic bliss and lost track of time. The tub's Jacuzzi setting massaged her tired body, and Minka could've pampered herself there for several more hours.

She decided against that. One couldn't while away the hours when there was work to be done. Laughing softly over the idea, Minka made a lazy effort to leave the tub. The bubbles hadn't completely dissolved, and they clung to her body even as the water sluiced down her belly and thighs. Stepping out of the tub, she discovered that the rugs delivered on their promise of plush comfort and warmth.

Relaxed and refreshed, Minka took a moment to admire herself in the big mirror.

"Guess I should've called first," said a husky voice behind her.

She turned on a dime, forgetting that she was only covered by quickly dissipating bubbles. Her total focus was now on Oliver Bauer leaning against the door frame.

Chapter 4

"Vectra, she—she gave me a key."

"That's obvious." Oliver's smirk seemed to elevate the usual roguish light in his eyes as he listened to Minka stammer her explanation.

"I was just taking a bath…"

"I can tell." The hungry intensity of his expression fused with something softer, more amused. He knew she was beyond nervous, and it was beyond endearing.

Minka responded with an absent nod. She was still too stunned by the fact that Oliver Bauer was actually there in the doorway to remember that she was still naked. The bubbles and water had long since evaporated.

"What are you doing here?" she asked.

His mouth twitched on the cusp of a grin, which he shielded by holding a hand to his jaw in the pretense of rubbing it. Once the need to smile had been somewhat stifled, he made an effort to reply. "I'll explain if you don't mind us continuing this downstairs? It's getting pretty hard for me to think the way I should."

When she continued to stare as if bewildered, Oliver took another pointed appraisal of her body. He began at the red-wine polish adorning her toes. The shade accentuated the dark chocolate flawlessness of her skin. What she lacked in height, she made up for in curves. His gaze settled to her chest—again. The firm, flawlessly dark globes heaved with an unknowing sensuality as she watched him with utter obliviousness.

Minka blinked slowly once, twice, as though she were rising out of a dreamy fog. At last her attention shifted, following the trail of Oliver's stare, and taking in her state of undress.

"Right." She sighed, then muttered an inaudible curse. She moved to the cabinets where she'd seen a collection of towels folded during her earlier inspection of the bath.

Clearing her head with a shake, she grabbed a towel. It wasn't a bath sheet, but it would do. Quickly she wrapped herself in it and turned.

Oliver Bauer was gone.

The aroma of brewing coffee stimulated Minka's nostrils as she crossed into the connecting bedroom suite. She'd left a robe on the bed, not bothering to carry it with her into the bath. Of course, then she hadn't been expecting that she'd be visited by her hostess's unfairly sexy older brother.

Those words, and all that they implied, echoed in her mind for a time. Minka gave another quick shake of her head in the hopes of warding off scorching images of what might have played out during their encounter.

The idea almost made her laugh. Anything between her and Oliver would definitely have to be tabled, no matter how much she'd love to explore it. The old saying about never mixing business with pleasure was popular for a reason. Such a rule had served her well, and she wasn't about to abandon it now. No matter how tempting it was to do so.

But he won't be business for long, Mink. You're about to be an ex-employee of Wilder, remember?

Her third head-clearing shake was accompanied by a fist to the mattress. Minka pushed herself to stand and took some calming breaths before leaving the bedroom. She followed her nose to the coffee and was halfway there when she realized she was still wearing the robe. Her plan had been to get dressed.

She paused halfway down the staircase and debated whether to get dressed when Oliver rounded the corner and sprinted up the stairway. He stopped a few steps shy of barreling into her. Bracing a hand to the wall, he fixed her with a guileless grin.

"I was just coming to ask how you take your coffee..." His baritone carried faint traces of breathlessness.

"What are you doing here?" Minka blurted the first thing that came to mind. She regarded the hand he offered with a mix of curiosity and hesitation. Yet she accepted his escort down the remaining stairs. She let him tug her hand over the crook of his arm as though it were a common occurrence between them.

"I always check out the place for Vectra whenever I'm in town," Oliver explained as they walked. "I have a key, and I knew she was heading off somewhere with Sim." He snorted. "But I knew she'd probably give me grief about checking in since she'd consider it one of my overprotective brother moves."

"Is that label accurate?" Minka queried.

"*I* don't think so." He shrugged. "But the one on the other side of the protection tends to feel differently about it."

Minka studied her fingers resting across his forearm. "So you believe her feelings are baseless?"

"She's my little sister."

"By eighteen months."

"It's my job."

"Because she's a woman."

"All right."

He owned the chauvinism with a coolness that would have had her bristling had he been any other man. He made her want to laugh instead. She couldn't help but wonder how infuriating her escort could be.

The aroma of brewing coffee grew sharper, and soon they were crossing the threshold into the kitchen. Like other rooms in the condo, the kitchen was vast. Furnished with state-of-the-art gadgetry and appliances, the kitchen was done in tones of walnut, mocha and beige, with splashes of cream and burgundy.

Minka thought the space had the same soothing allure as the rest of the house. Oliver pulled out one of the wrought iron stools from the large cooking island. Once Minka was settled, he went to the cabinet near the towering black fridge and selected mugs.

Minka watched while he labored over choosing the mugs. "It's all right, you know? You didn't do anything wrong. I'm fine. You don't have to stick around to make sure I'm not about to jump out of my skin."

"Well, we can't have that, can we?" Oliver turned with the two mugs he'd deemed appropriate for their coffee break. His eyes raked her skin.

"I know you're okay." He poured the coffee. "Maybe *I'm* the one about to jump out of my skin over the thought that I could have stumbled in on my *sister* in *her* bathwater." He shivered as if truly mortified by the idea.

The kitchen echoed with the sounds of Minka's laughter.

Oliver kept his eyes on the mugs, but the smile curving his lips hinted that he highly approved of her reaction. It took Minka quite a few tries to stifle her hearty laughter.

"Sorry."

"What for?" He shrugged.

Minka shook her head. "You sounded so horrified just now, and I—I shouldn't offend you by making light of it." Laughter hovered just below her words.

"Well, hell, Minka, it's a horrifying thought." He shivered again.

The gesture threatened to send Minka back into laughter.

"You didn't offend me. It's never offensive to hear a beautiful woman laugh."

The confession surprised her, and she stared at him while absorbing it.

"How do you take it?"

She couldn't answer—the question rendered her just as immobile as his confession.

"Minka? How do you take your coffee?"

"Sweet." *Jeez, Mink, don't make an even bigger fool of yourself.* "Sugar and cream," she rephrased.

Oliver seemed to think nothing of the manner in which she delivered her responses. He dutifully prepared the beverage and then passed her the mug, while blowing across the surface of his own unsweetened black. For a time, they enjoyed sips from their mugs in silence.

"Minka?" Oliver didn't lift his gaze from the mug he held. "What you said about not jumping out of your skin."

Minka nodded. "Yes," she said, noticing he was looking elsewhere.

"What I'm about to tell you might change that."

"Okay." She cupped the mug in her hands, needing the warmth it provided.

"I want to know what you're like in bed." He looked at her then.

She couldn't close her mouth. "Oliver…" was the best she could manage after a few seconds.

"Sorry." He didn't look at all apologetic. "I've always had a problem with *not* beating around the bush. Truth is, I'm very proud of myself for not telling you this the first night I met you."

Minka finally got around to swallowing. "Is that kind of straightforwardness what makes you so successful with women?"

His smile was one of surprised curiosity. "How do you know I'm successful with women?"

"Kind of hard not to know." Minka focused on her coffee again. "Anyone watching you at dinner the other night could tell you've got no shortcomings in that area—almost every woman in the room made a point of stopping by to speak to you."

"I know a lot of women intimately, Minka, that's true."

"And do you make a point of 'not beating around the bush' with every woman you know?"

"I've never said what I just told you to another woman." His tone registered as totally sincere.

Minka sipped her coffee in hopes of quelling her laughter.

"You don't believe me?" His gaze fell to her smiling mouth.

"Well, since we're being straightforward." She looked at him. "No, not at all."

Oliver dissolved into laughter. "I didn't say I'd never *thought it* about another woman, but I've never *told* another woman that."

"Ah…" Minka propped her chin with her hand. "You need to be more vocal with the clueless ones, huh?" She was teasing, but some of her playfulness eased when she saw his expression change. "Oliver…?"

"I don't know why I told you that." He gave a half shrug. "Maybe I just didn't want there to be any confusion."

"And you think there would be?"

Again, he shrugged, this time giving his mug a turn, slightly disturbing its contents. "There usually tends to be."

"You're right." She returned her focus to her mug too. "That's why I never sleep with men I know through business."

"Have there been many of those?"

"A couple." She continued to study her mug. "Those

experiences have been enough for me to turn down future opportunities that present themselves."

"Future opportunities?"

"Mr. Bauer." She smiled, knowing full well what he was asking. "Surely you're not curious about how many men I've slept with?"

"Men are always curious about how many men a woman has slept with, especially a woman they're interested in."

"You included?"

He appeared thoughtful. "A week ago, my answer would have been 'no,' as I've never been interested enough to care."

Dark eyes sparkled with curious disbelief. "And now?" She gave an airy wave. "Suddenly that's changed?"

"Well I'm not in the habit of spending so much time talking to any woman, unless it's business related."

"Excuse me." She blurted a laugh. "But that's not saying much for your wooing skills."

"I won't argue that." He raised his hands in surrender. "But in my defense, you'd be surprised by what a few witty remarks, reservations at the best restaurants and a few nice cars can do for a guy's sex life."

Minka's gaze took a slow perusal of the powerful cords of muscle lining his exposed forearms. "You seem like the kind of man who'd be about more than that."

"Sometimes I think I might be."

"Why the hesitation?"

"No reason to be fully committed to it, I guess."

"Is commitment an issue for you?"

He smiled. "An issue…that's a funny way to put it."

"Is it? Does it scare you?"

"It's got me more curious lately."

She gave a sage nod. "Why do you think that is?" She was vaguely aware that she'd reverted back to sighing her words again. She didn't care. His eyes were amazing. The shade—such a captivating light brown—made looking away impossible.

"I want to know what makes perfectly rational people risk their sanity for something so fleeting," he confessed.

"It's interesting you feel that way. According to Vectra, your parents had a very happy, long marriage."

"Not long enough. My dad wanted forever." Oliver sighed, rubbing his fingers through his hair again. "We thought he'd kill himself when our mother died. Loving someone to the point of wanting to kill yourself if you lost them…? I don't know what I think of that. Before I saw you running out of my sister's house the other morning, I'd never given any of it a second thought."

"Oliver…what are you…what are you trying to say?"

"I'm saying that when I saw you I wanted to take you to bed, but I want things like that on the regular." He grimaced over the admission. "But it was only with you that I wondered what it might be like to take you to bed every night."

"Oliver…" She straightened. "You—you don't know me."

"Will you let me change that?"

Minka seemed to snap out of her dreamy haze then. "It will change—we're going to be around each other for weeks if Austin Sharpe has his way." She laughed, hoping to bring lightness to the moment. She eased off the chair to retrieve the coffeepot for a refill. When she turned after adding sugar and cream, he was right behind her.

"This isn't about business," he said.

"Oliver, it's *always* about business. *This*, *we*, it wouldn't be a good idea."

He smiled, apparently not agreeing with the prediction. "It's still early, yet."

"Oliver…" Minka let her words drift into silence, at a total loss. He took her hand, and she blinked when she felt cold metal against her palm. She saw the key, and the exasperation in her gaze turned to curiosity.

"You shouldn't have to worry about me just dropping over whenever I feel like it."

She laughed, a great deal of her apprehension easing. "It's your sister's place, Oliver."

"It's yours while you're in Miami. Besides…" His light eyes pooled to a bolder hue. "I've never been any good with temptation." He held her cheek, thumb brushing her high cheekbone. Nodding approvingly, he looked as though his expectations had not only been reached, but exceeded. He issued her a quiet good-night before leaving.

"I'd suggest limiting it to members of the senior executive staff and the board."

Austin Sharpe nodded at Minka's suggestion just as his brows rose to acknowledge a raised hand from a member of his staff. "Yeah, Barry?"

"It says here that Gallery V can handle four times as many people," Barry Tomkin read from a page he'd pulled from the portfolio.

"Barry, keep in mind that we'll be there too." Minka smiled patiently at Sharpe's Marketing VP. "Addition-

ally, we want the focus to be on the art, which is the fa-
cilities your boss wants the clients to lease or purchase.
The emphasis shouldn't be on how packed the house is.
Though I think we could have a standby list of guests
to be granted last-minute admittance. A line of waiting
guests might look good for the event." She gave Austin
an indulgent smile. "Just my two cents."

"It's a lot more than that." Austin returned a grin.
"Guys, Ms. Gerald has put together some of the biggest
functions out West for one of the largest firms in the
nation. If there's anyone's input I value most, it's hers."

Several men at the table shifted in their seats, yet regarded Minka with curiosity, grudging admiration and
something more primal.

"Meeting adjourned. Minka? Stay a second," Austin requested.

When they were alone, Minka said, "I'm not out to
be the teacher's pet."

"Ah!" Austin waved. "It's good for them to see that
they aren't always going to command the meetings."

"Well, this preliminary meeting was a good idea."
Minka began to pack her things. "I only hope the other
kids remember how to play nice once teacher leaves
the class."

"None of them can argue with your track record,
Minka." Austin knocked the table with a decisive fist.

"I'll take your word for it." Minka finished packing.
"The pieces will be arranged at the gallery's discretion,
but I'd like to see the office space firsthand, if we could
arrange that before the event."

"Fine idea—you can head out whenever you're ready.
I'll make sure a car is available."

"Sounds good." Minka stood, smiling when Austin

followed suit. "We're still meeting with members of the executive staff for dinner, right?"

"That's still the plan."

"See you tonight, then." She headed off.

Austin reclaimed his seat and took time to admire Minka making her way out of the restaurant where she'd met him and his team for breakfast. He was still in the midst of admiring her departing figure when Oliver arrived.

"Oli! Didn't think you'd be able to make it this morning."

Oliver inclined his head toward Minka. "How long have you known her?" He took a seat at the square glass table.

"Let's see." Austin leaned back in his chair. "She worked for Sim long before I became a client."

"She's very on top of her game," Oliver noted.

"Damn right she is. No one can deny that."

"Coffee—black," Oliver told the waiter who'd approached. "Guess it's difficult for her to be taken seriously, looking the way she does."

"Hmph—all that knowledge coming from someone so gorgeous." Austin shook his head. "It stirs a man in the nicest way possible." He noticed Oliver's tight, disapproving expression and smiled. "Forget about Minka Gerald, my friend. You may be the most successful ladies' man I know, but no way will you get that woman to deviate from that code of hers. Not mixing business with pleasure? It's like gospel to her."

"Yeah." Oliver shifted in the chair he'd taken. "I got that part loud and clear."

"But you believe you're the guy she'd break her own rule for, huh?"

"I'm the *last* guy she should break it for."

"Mmm…and why do I have the feeling you'll try to make it happen anyway?" Austin began to laugh.

Oliver joined in soon after.

Chapter 5

Minka made a quick stop by Gallery V. Once a few members of the staff discovered where she was going, they asked to come along. Minka was glad for the company, especially once they were well into the drive to the business park.

The beauty of South Beach wasn't lost on the passengers inside the Mercedes limo Austin Sharpe had secured for the trip. Vectra Bauer's gallery manager, acquisitions chief and event planner—all Florida natives—entertained Minka with stories of jockeying for camera time on *Miami Vice* back in the eighties. The conversation was so colorful that Minka almost hated to see it come to an end when they arrived at the site.

It was a breathtaking property with a backyard view of the Atlantic. Minka and the Gallery V workers parted ways soon after clearing the courtyard.

She was quietly appraising a row of office cottages spanning the southern end of the park when her phone interrupted her.

"This is Minka," she answered after digging the mobile from her fuchsia tote. "Hello?" she said again when her earlier greeting went unreturned.

"Hello?" She pulled the phone away to ensure the call was still connected.

"Quite a place, huh?"

Minka heard the voice behind her and turned to find a rail-thin redhead walking toward her. "It is," she agreed, smiling as she tossed the phone back into the depths of her bag.

"Hildy Craft, site supervisor." The redhead extended a hand.

"Minka Gerald, I'm with Wilder" she returned.

Hildy nodded. "I know. Mr. Sharpe said you were coming over." Her face turned toward the courtyard. "Some place, huh? The guy's really a genius, isn't he?"

"Definitely." Minka fell in step with the other woman. "Everyone knows what an open thinker Austin is—this proves it."

Hildy laughed. "Yeah, Mr. Sharpe's a genius in his own right, but I was talking about Oliver."

"Oh—agreed, agreed. It's not everyone who's got such an eye for real-estate potential."

"True." Hildy held her hands clasped behind her back as she walked. "But in Oliver's case, it's about more than spotting a piece of land. It's one of the things that makes Bauer D so successful—a passion for architecture."

Minka blinked, her steps slowing. "Are you saying Oliver Bauer is the architect who designed this place?"

"Indeed he is." Hildy beamed. "If Oliver can't envision the place he actually wants on the property, then he doesn't go after it."

"You sound impressed," Minka noted, though she felt exactly the same.

Hildy shrugged. "It's hard not to be. The man's a genius, and don't get me started on his looks." Her steps slowed and she looked at Minka. "Have you met him?"

Minka smiled. "I have."

Hildy gave a wave. "Then there's no need for an introduction."

Minka discovered that Hildy had led her right to Oliver's office. At least, she assumed that's where they were.

"Thanks for bringing her to me, Hildy." He read Minka's curious stare with ease. "I just grabbed an office to work from while we cover our bases with this gallery thing," he explained once the site manager had walked off. "Have you seen it all?"

"I thought I had." She gave him a measured look. "So you designed this place, huh?"

He gave a modest shrug. "Just a lil' somethin' I picked up."

"Well, you picked it up very well." Minka cast an appraising eye around the room.

"Thanks." He sounded preoccupied. "Minka, um…" He waited for her to finish her survey of the room. "About yesterday—"

"Oliver, really, it's fine," She gave him a patient smile. "You've got every right to check in on your sister's place."

"Thanks, but I…I was talking about what happened after that. I shouldn't have come on as strong as I did."

She flashed a brilliant smile, hoping to make light of the moment. "I've never seen coming on strong done so smoothly." Her smile intensified when he burst into laughter.

"Would you at least let me make it up to you with dinner?" he asked, once his laughter subsided.

"It's fine, really. You don't have to do that—" She stopped short as he moved to stand close to her.

"I know I don't have to, but I want to. Very much."

"Oliver…"

"I know we can't break your rule."

She caught the amusement underscoring his words. "It's a very good rule."

"So? Would you be breaking any part of it by having dinner with me?"

"No," she acknowledged with a smile, all the while calling herself an idiot for hedging.

It was Miami. She'd practically been ordered to have fun. *He* was gorgeous, and hell…it wasn't like they'd see each other once the project was over anyway. Aside from a possible wedding between Qasim and Vectra, she would probably never run into Oliver Bauer again. Not as a business associate anyway. He was business now, but he wouldn't be forever.

Oliver was wearing an adorably skeptical expression. "Does that *no* mean you're willing to join me?"

She nodded. "I'm willing to join you. What have you got in mind?"

"Whatever it is, I'll make it good. Chances are it'll be my only time to impress you."

"Trust me, you've already done that on the strength of this place alone." She gestured around the large room.

"It's a good thing Austin has a tour scheduled among

the list of events." She studied the lofty ceiling and the smooth dark oak paneling that supported potted ferns of varying sizes. "Your photographers have a great eye, Oliver, but their work has nothing on the real thing." She looked at him. "You're very talented."

"Thank you, Minka." He was undoubtedly pleased by her compliment. He suddenly cleared his throat, looking away as though his expression may have revealed too much. "Was there anything else you needed to see while you're here?"

"Well, I saw quite a bit on my way in with Vectra's staff." She looked askance at the door. "They're probably wondering where I am. We hadn't planned to stay very long."

"They're fine. Hildy will make sure they get back to the city all right."

"Ah…so that's why she disappeared. Is she a mind reader as well as an enthusiastic supporter of your work?"

A guilty smile narrowed Oliver's beautiful stare. "I might've given her a little instruction when she told me you were here."

Minka didn't know what to say to that, so she turned her focus to the room again.

"Minka, you should know that I have a habit of coming on strong when something appeals to me, but you don't have to be afraid of me."

She was painstakingly studying the patterns crafted into the glass skylights on the ceiling. She heard his voice very close, very…soft. When she turned, he was right there, looking adorable and wholly concerned that she feared him.

But her expression was soft, bordering on amused. "Oliver that—that's crazy. You've done nothing to—"

His head dipped, and he was kissing her, his tongue plundering, exploring, discovering. Minka responded with a moan that held tones of surprise and need. She wasn't sure what to do with her hands, but then he took possession of her wrists. He held them fast as he tugged her deeper into the kiss.

The gesture wasn't overpowering—it teased. At first, Minka had been too stunned to respond, but his tongue continued to tantalize hers, thrusting and withdrawing during its hearty sampling of her mouth. Minka steadily retreated from her long-standing rule. Such a kiss was not a thing to be resisted, and she no longer had the will to say no.

She flexed her fingers, her wrists still commanded by his grip. She was barely able to grab a corner of the charcoal-brown jacket he wore over a shirt a few shades lighter. Open at the collar, the shirt revealed strong chords of muscle lining his neck.

Moaning anew, Minka committed to the kiss, her tongue accepting his invitation to play. She was seconds from demanding he release her wrists, when he released her from the kiss altogether. She whimpered in sheer disappointment.

Oliver raised his head a fraction and smiled adoringly into Minka's upturned face. Her eyes were still closed, and she seemed to be edging closer in a silent request for more.

"How about now?" He felt a stab of something heated and basic when she looked at him with her dark riveting eyes.

"How about now, what?"

She purred the words, which made him laugh. He captured a glimpse of what had, until then, eluded him—what laughter felt like when it was brought on by happiness.

Minka's expression cleared as though she were waking from a dream. Oliver dropped a kiss to the corner of her mouth before she could begin to overthink what had just happened. Suddenly, his phone rang.

"Yeah?"

Minka turned away while Oliver handled his call, but she didn't get far. He captured the sleeve of the emerald-green blouson dress she sported, keeping her in place. The call ended after only a few seconds.

"Your ride's ready," he said.

Minka blinked, working hard not to appear too relieved—or too disappointed—by the news.

"Tonight at seven." It wasn't a question.

"Tonight at seven," she confirmed anyway.

All the while, Minka wondered what he would have thought if she'd asked to stay in.

Jeez, Mink, it was only a kiss!

But it had been a long time since she'd had one that affecting. Oliver Bauer was certainly a man of many talents—that was a distinct certainty.

She managed to dismiss Oliver and his persuasive presence from her mind as she focused on choosing an outfit for dinner. He hadn't mentioned anything else being on the agenda, but she wondered if his kiss was a promise of things to come.

Again, Minka shook her head for clarity. She was surprised to find that she had, in fact, selected a not-too-shabby outfit for the evening. The gold toga dress was trendy yet elegant. The airy fabric was a gorgeous blend of chiffon and silk, and the color was flattering to her deep skin tone. Strappy heeled sandals, the same color as the dress, waited near the sofa in the living room for her to slip into.

She was making the decision to leave her hair loose and bouncing around her face, when the phone rang. She didn't rush to answer. She'd left her cell phone upstairs while she stood preening before the downstairs mirror. Finally, she grabbed the cordless in the living room on the fourth ring.

"Vectra Bauer's residence." Minka took the phone back with her to the mirror and resumed teasing the loose curls of her bob.

"Hello?" Her voice, polite yet inquiring, generated no response. "Hello?" She lost interest in her reflection and left the mirror with the phone still clutched to her ear. Whoever was waiting silently on the other end of the line had no intention of responding. Minka waited, holding her breath.

She took small comfort in the fact that her mysterious caller's patience ran out before hers. The dial tone sounded about two minutes after she'd gone quiet. Quickly, she checked the phone directory, not surprised to find the number was blocked.

Minka set aside the house phone then ran upstairs to get her cell phone from the nightstand in the guest bedroom. She made a quick search through the call log and discovered that the previous three calls she'd answered and gotten no reply from had also come from blocked numbers. She recapped the calls she'd gotten and tried to determine if there had been any clues the caller left about his or her identity. The caller had been careful.

She took another look through the phone, scrolling through her contacts and finding the one she wanted. She hesitated. This could be a coincidence, after all. People dialed wrong numbers all the time, didn't they? No need to go to great lengths to track down the person.

The bell rang, and Minka accepted that as her answer. She returned the phone to her evening bag, taking it with her as she hurried downstairs.

She threw the door open, happy that Oliver was early. She'd need his easy company to dismiss her sudden dread.

It wasn't Oliver Bauer on the other side of the door.

"Will?"

Will Lloyd's gaze was flat, even when it repeatedly raked Minka's curvy frame.

"Minka…" His purr lent insight to his mood.

Minka kept a tight rein on her courage and her place at the front door. "What do you want?"

"Let me in."

"I'm on my way out."

"I don't think so. This is important."

"I disagree, since you didn't think it was important enough to tell me about when you called." She pretended to ponder. "Five times now, I think? Including your call here a few minutes ago."

He smiled. "No idea what you're talking about."

"What do you want?"

"To come inside."

"Forget it."

"I was given a raw deal, Mink."

"You gave *yourself* that deal." She regarded him reproachfully. "Qasim was nothing but kind to you, even when he knew you weren't worth the effort."

"And now he won't even take my calls."

"You should be praising Sim for not calling someone to take you to jail." She seethed over the man's nerve.

Will didn't seem agitated by her words. "I guess that's what you were hoping for. What was it, Mink? Jealous because Sim wasn't giving you enough attention? Course you can't blame the guy. That Vectra Bauer is one sweet piece. Sim's always been too much of a straight arrow, though. Me? I'd have taken you both."

Minka's smile gained definition the longer Will rambled. When he finished, she nodded past his shoulder and waited for him to turn.

"Will Lloyd, this is Oliver Bauer. Vectra's brother," she tacked on with sickly sweetness.

Minka took great delight in watching the man swallow uneasily.

Oliver fixed Minka with an unwavering look. "Thought you were all mine tonight."

"I am—I…um—I only need to put on my shoes. Will just stopped by to—" She faked a confused look. "Will, why'd you say you stopped by?"

Suddenly a lot less confident, Will cleared his throat and backed away from the front door. "It can wait. Nice to meet you." He scarcely glanced in Oliver's direction as he edged past and hurried down the brick drive.

"Should my fist and his jaw be getting acquainted?" Oliver's gaze followed Will Lloyd's departing figure.

"Don't waste your time." Minka tugged on his jacket lapel, urging him inside.

Oliver shut the front door. "Who is he?" He followed Minka into the living room.

"Used to work for Wilder. Qasim fired him, breach

of contract or something. Only a select few know that it was really embezzlement."

"Wait, Vectra told me something about this. Was the guy involved with Sim's charity?"

"That's him." Minka sat on the sofa near her shoes. "Guess he thought he was entitled to a bigger piece of the pie, since he once saved Qasim's life."

Oliver blurted a laugh and hiked a thumb over his shoulder. "*That* guy?" He thought of Will Lloyd cowering before him a few moments earlier. Humor and disbelief illuminated his handsome features.

"That guy." Minka's expression was just as bright, but she quickly sobered. "It happened when they were in the army."

Nodding, Oliver sobered as well. He leaned against a pine bookshelf and watched as Minka slipped on one of the strappy, spiked heels.

Any lingering waves of amusement lost their grip—his focus was on her slipping into the sandals. As if drawn by some unseen force, he closed the distance between them.

"Help with that?" he asked when she looked up. He waved toward the shoe she was trying to fasten.

Minka moved her hands, silently accepting the offer. He knelt before her, and for a while Minka wondered if he had any plans to fasten her shoe at all.

Oliver relished the chance to simply admire her legs up close. He began to secure the shoes to her feet, and then paused again to admire one at length. He extended her leg and raked his stare along the dark shapely limb made even more provocative by the chic sandal.

Minka pressed her lips together to stifle a sudden desire to moan. Parts of her clenched, throbbing for his touch. When Oliver released her leg, disappointment and hope surged at once. When he stood, hope faded.

"Are we ready?" He was squeezing her hand, urging her to stand.

To hell with it, she thought. "Would you think less of me if I said no?"

Oliver smiled, but the gesture didn't quite reach his amazing eyes. "You'll want to be careful about what you say to me, Ms. Gerald."

"Oh? Are the consequences that awful?" Her heart flipped as his expression intensified.

"The consequences aren't awful, but they have the potential to be obscenely demanding."

"Demanding?"

"Obscenely."

She observed him more astutely. "You talk a good game, Oliver."

He stepped within an inch of her. "I'm a man of my word. You'll want to remember that."

He backed off, and only then did Minka discover she was holding her breath.

"Mink?"

She saw him wave a hand to usher her toward the front. She pulled a hand through her hair, not caring that he saw how off-kilter she was. Praying her heels wouldn't let her down, she moved toward the front door.

Chapter 6

The very last thing on Minka's mind was dinner, but that changed by the time one of the valets escorted her from the passenger side of Oliver's rented SUV.

Their reservations had been for Keene's. The popular steakhouse was as known and loved for its choice cuts of beef as it was for the jazz and blues artists who performed live every night. It was about a forty-minute ride from Vectra's—enough time to put Minka's thoughts back to eating.

Well…that wasn't completely accurate. Her appetite may have taken command of her thoughts a time or two, but never long enough to forget the little repartee between her and Oliver before they left the condo. She had been more honest than she'd ever intended, but now it was done and she couldn't go back and make him forget what she'd said.

"Mink?"

She heard the quiet timbre of his voice, but didn't immediately lock on to the fact that he was calling her name until he leaned across the table to snap his fingers before her face. She saw the playfulness in his gaze and realized the waiter was at the table.

"Charlie wants to know what you'd like to drink, babe."

"Sorry." Minka cleared her throat. "Champagne cocktail, please."

Oliver nodded to send the waiter on his way. "You want to talk to me, or is your daydreaming more fun?"

Minka decided to be forthcoming again. "My daydream was about you...us...what happened before we left. I gave you no indication that I wanted to leave even after you told me there would be consequences—obscenely demanding ones..."

"You're right." Oliver relaxed back against the cushioned armchair at the intimate table. "I guess there's just something...that disturbs me about having sex in my little sister's house."

Minka couldn't resist a quick burst of laughter. "It's nice you guys are so close."

He shrugged. "She can be aggravating as hell, but I love her. She's the only one who doesn't mind telling me when I'm being a jackass."

Minka contained her laughter as the waiter returned with her champagne cocktail and a Sam Adams for Oliver. "Beer drinker," she mused watching him tip the liquid into a chilled mug. "That's interesting, considering your family's business is wine."

Oliver kept his gaze on the mug. "Just because you make bread doesn't mean you can't eat cake."

Minka scrunched her nose in a playful gesture. "That's not a very good analogy."

"You don't think so?" He faked being taken aback. "Hmph, that one usually gets me a lot of laughs. Folks always notice when I've got a drink in my hands that isn't a Carro wine."

Minka sipped her cocktail and took time to enjoy the restaurant's atmosphere. Keene's had a rugged saloon allure that was smoothed out at the edges by the ease and sensuality of the jazzy, bluesy aura that seemed to permeate the air like something tangible. It was a soft-lit establishment which lent something distinctly romantic to its atmosphere—an element made more evocative by her present company.

She was looking down at the lower level of the dining room. Oliver had arranged for them to have a table with a direct view of the stage, but they could also turn and be dazzled by the beautiful excess of South Beach from the tall windows along the opposing wall of the room.

"Oliver?"

"Mmm…"

Minka smiled, loving the lazy hum of his voice. Apparently, he was as relaxed by the atmosphere as she. "What was it like for you growing up around all this?" She didn't look away from the stage until she'd posed her question. "Carro," she clarified. "Your parents accomplished a lot, and you're meant to take it over some day. That's a lot on a kid's shoulders, don't you think?"

Oliver's brows rose as he considered her question. "Could be."

"What do you think that does to a kid?"

"I don't know." He straightened in his chair and focused on his beer mug again. "Guess it'd make 'em strong. Or psychotic."

"Which one did it make you?"

"Well, me, personally, I think it's good to have a little of both." He laughed and she joined in.

The waiter returned for their dinner orders and, once he'd left with the requests, Oliver and Minka talked about everything, from musical interests to the hottest spots for San Francisco nightlife. When Minka admitted that she was woefully lacking on the subject of nightlife, in San Francisco or anyplace else, Oliver told her that was a shame.

Their meals arrived, and hearty steaks were the stars of both entrées. Minka's was a petite sirloin while Oliver dug into a thick T-bone. They ate in relaxed silence, only speaking to ask for pepper, sauce, or honey butter for their potatoes. Gradually, conversation resumed.

"You work too hard not to have a little fun, you know?"

"Yeah, well." Minka dabbed a napkin corner to her mouth. "My boss is the demanding type."

Oliver smiled over the dig at Qasim. "I don't think you'd have a problem if he was, but I don't think he's quite as demanding as you make him out to be."

"And how would you know?" She laughed.

"I'm very observant." He shrugged and swigged from his second Sam Adams. "Triply so, being an architect, a boss and a big brother. But you don't strike me as the type with a hearty social life."

"Thanks a lot."

Her sarcasm resulted in a cool smile from Oliver. "You know that's not what I meant."

"So what type do I strike you as?" She made a show of relaxing in the cushioned, pine-framed chair.

Oliver clearly appreciated the sight of her moving around in the roomy chair. "You strike me as the type that keeps her social life intimate with only room for yourself and one other."

Minka raised her brows as though she'd been impressed by his perceptiveness. "A woman has to be careful of how much people know about her social life. Such things don't get us the pats on the back that men enjoy." Some of the cool amusement left her face. "A woman can expect innuendo, spite, ridicule, usually from other women."

"Did that happen to you?" He told himself to unclench the fist he'd drawn, realizing he'd clenched it as she'd spoken. Imagining her going through such ugliness stirred what was usually a very slow-to-heat temper.

Minka's smile was reflective and sad. "Not me, but I know someone who has and I learned. I learned very well."

Oliver caught the waiter's eye, raised two fingers indicating the request for fresh drinks. "So you lock yourself away as a result of that?"

"I don't lock myself away, Oliver. I'm just very careful about who I give my key to."

"Why'd you decide to share it with me?"

Minka shook her head. "That wasn't my intention."

"But I was just so persuasive, right?"

"That too."

"What else? Honestly, Minka."

"It's Miami."

"Right." He nodded as though he'd predicted the answer. "So you decided to give in to a fling while you're here?"

"One that you seemed to have no problem taking part in." Minka caught the terseness in his tone and responded in kind. "I want to know what you're like in bed." She gave him the words he'd said to her less than two days ago. She noticed the slight flare of his nostrils and knew her intrigue had heightened. Surely he wasn't about to deny saying it? Or maybe he was angry at having his words thrown back at him.

It was neither.

Oliver was angry, but for an entirely different reason. "So you took my words to mean that I was in the market for a fling as well."

She smiled. "Those words are usually part of the conversation when people talk about flings."

"Yes, but *people* weren't talking about flings, Minka. *You* were talking about flings."

"Oliver…" Some of the curiosity gave way to distinct confusion. "I'm…sorry? I guess I misunderstood."

"I'm the one who should apologize." Sincerity was evident on his handsome face. "I wasn't very clear, was I?"

She shook her head but smiled. "I thought you were very clear."

"Not if you think all I wanted from you is one night."

"Well, I'd love to see you more than once while we're in Miami."

"I want to see you in Miami and after Miami."

"Oliver, you…" She blinked, straightened a bit in her chair. "You don't mean we…you want to see me in San Francisco?"

"We both live there, don't we?"

"Exactly." She breathed out the word on a chord of laughter. "Oliver it's too—I—I can't do that. Not there. This." She gave a pointed look around the dining room. "All I can give you is here in Miami. If you think about it, you'll see I'm right."

Oliver signaled for the waiter again. "Check," he said when the man got within earshot of the table.

Minka tapped her fingers against the table and watched the beautiful evening go straight down the disposal like a chunk of rotting garbage. "Oliver, talk to me. Please?" She urged when he seemed set on ignoring her.

He reached for his wallet in preparation for the check's arrival. He sat quietly but for the impatient tapping of his fingers to the table's surface.

Minka reached over to put her hand atop his. "Oliver—"

He grabbed her hand, squeezed. "You're better than some fling, some one-night stand that doesn't mean anything."

Minka didn't know that she'd ever felt so stunned. She opened her mouth, closed it, shook her head and then repeated the process. Her head seemed to throb with questions, but she couldn't seem to find the words to express even one of them.

Oliver could see her surprise, could tell that his words had stunned and staggered. The emotions echoed inside him too. Where the hell had that come from? He bowed his head, taking a hand through the wealth of brown curls adorning his head.

It was true. She deserved more than some one-night stand that didn't mean anything. Hell yes, she did. Was he the one to give that to her though? Him? The guy who didn't even believe in spending the night when he took a woman to bed? *That guy?* That guy wasn't the one who could pull off something like that. And he sure as hell wasn't the one who deserved a beautiful gem like Minka Gerald. *But don't you want to be?*

The waiter arrived with the check, and Oliver stood and passed the man a wad of cash.

"Oliver, please," Minka urged again, once the waiter had bid them good-night.

Oliver walked around to Minka's side of the table and helped her from her chair. They left the restaurant, leaving behind the aroma of good food, the chorus of hearty conversation and the swell of infectious music.

Saint Helena, CA

Vectra finally returned to the main house after a long day tending to last-minute vineyard issues before taking her trip with Qasim. She was celebrating the fact that she was almost done with her packing when the house line buzzed unexpectedly.

Head housekeeper Charlotte Sweeny informed Vectra that she was needed out at the west vineyard. She slipped on her sneakers, grabbed her keys and was zooming off to the requested spot in one of the property Jeeps in less than five minutes.

By the time she'd arrived, a crowd had gathered along the main road that branched off into a series of narrow secondary roads leading deeper into the east vineyard.

"Ah, jeez…" she groaned, able to make out the drawn, unreadable looks some of the men wore. She pulled to a stop where they'd gathered. Readying herself for the catastrophe that would surely put the kibosh on her vacation, she left the Jeep.

"Charlotte said you guys needed me out here ASAP—what's up?" Vectra watched the foreman, Kurt Zigler, step forward.

The man looked more harried than usual as he took off his cap and held it near his forehead while scratching at thinning black curls near his temple. "Sorry to call you back out, Vectra, but we've got a disturbance blocking the road about half a mile in," Kurt explained.

"What kind of disturbance?" Her usually dependable staff didn't have many such upsets. "Is there something wrong with the crop?"

"Not exactly."

Vectra looked skeptical. "Have you guys even seen this disturbance?"

"Well, uh." Kurt shared a quick look with his colleagues. "We were told it was private."

"Told it was private?" Vectra fisted her hands to her hips. "Kurt—"

"Now, just hold on." Kurt waved both hands defensively. "We're sorry, but that's what he said."

"He? Does *he* know this is private property?"

Kurt shrugged a beefy shoulder. "No offense, Vectra, but the guy didn't act like he gave a crap about that."

"Oh, he didn't?" Her voice was deceptively cool. "Well, let's see if he gives a crap about this."

The men watched their boss return to the Jeep, which roared to life in seconds. Vectra hit the gas hard and sped down the road where the "disturbance" lay.

She'd driven less than half a mile when her scowl

cleared. Her mouth fell open once more, not in exasperation, but captivation.

A small round table was covered by a gold cloth, the edges of which flared against a cool breeze. The table was situated in the middle of the road as though it had every right to be there. Adorning the table was a candelabrum gleaming with flickering candles that were vibrant against the darkening evening backdrop.

Round silver covers of varying sizes shielded at least six dishes. As stunning a sight as it was, what held Vectra truly captivated was Qasim standing in the midst of it all.

Slowly, dazedly, she shut off the ignition and left the Jeep. Qasim, his strikingly gorgeous face unreadable, moved toward her. Vectra was still so in awe of the moment, that she didn't hear the commotion of her staff as Jeeps pulled up to witness the scene. Almost the entire vineyard staff had gathered.

"What are you doing here?" Vectra's words were slow, her manner still stunned when she met him just a few feet from the table.

Qasim offered an encouraging smile. "What'd you hear?"

"That someone was causing a disturbance."

Qasim nodded his agreement. "I guess there could be one of those if I don't get what I want."

"And, uh…" Vectra smoothed her hands over her arms and gave herself a light squeeze. "What do you want?"

Sim glanced toward the table. "What does it look like?"

"Dinner?" She blurted.

"That a problem?"

"No, but…here?"

He smiled. "I've thought about this since we were out here a few months back."

Vectra remembered. It was the first time they had exchanged *I love you*s.

"You could've told me," she said.

He chuckled, helping her into one of the cushioned chairs at the table. "Then that would've spoiled the surprise."

"At least then I could've dressed for the occasion." She smiled up at him. "And there wouldn't have been any expectations of a disturbance."

"Not so fast, Ms. Bauer. I still haven't gotten everything I want."

Before she could ask, he was plucking a small box from the table and kneeling before her chair. Vectra tuned in to the crowd behind her, hearing gasps, giggles and several grunts of approval. Her heart lifted, and her breath caught.

"Vectra…you've been my friend and now my best friend," he said. "I know we should be waiting, but I really need you to be my wife."

"Sim…"

He nodded, absorbing the way she sighed his name. "You don't have to give me an answer right—"

"Yes."

He inhaled sharply when the word touched his ears. "Yes?"

"Yes, Qasim. I want to be your wife." Vectra leaned closer to gaze directly into his eyes. "I want to be your wife very much."

Qasim closed his eyes, resting his forehead to Vectra's knee for just a moment before he gathered her close and lifted her from the chair.

The hushed silence of the crowd became cheers and cries of congratulations.

Minka didn't expect that Oliver would help her from the car, much less escort her back into the condo, when the SUV pulled to a smooth stop in the driveway. But he did. While he may've been a ladies' man of the most supreme variety, Oliver Bauer somehow managed to maintain the distinct air of a gentleman.

Their trip from the restaurant had passed without conversation. Neither of them sang along to the string of popular classics playing on the old-school R&B station they'd enjoyed during the drive earlier that night.

"Oliver, wait. Please?" Minka held her tongue until they were back inside the condo. Oliver was giving the place a thorough, yet efficient, check and then making his way back to the front door. She clutched her hands when his departure slowed.

"I'm very sorry about this, Oliver. I'd like for you to believe that. I shouldn't have made light of what you said before. I really thought we were on the same page there. I'm sorry I offended you. Just don't leave angry."

Oliver redirected his path and walked toward the living room while Minka made her argument.

She stopped, not knowing what else to say to close the void her words had produced.

"So you're telling me that I can stay as long as I'm angry?"

His words stopped her, but then she smiled.

"Sure." Oliver nodded and paced the room for a few

moments. His steps brought him closer to where Minka stood near the room's entryway. Her breath hitched, yet Minka forced down any reaction that hinted at her wantonness. The man had the ability to bring about that reaction with little more than a look. Promptly, Minka reminded herself that such a reaction was what had ruined a perfectly enjoyable evening.

She felt herself retreating and realized Oliver was nearly in front of her. She took a few steps back, and her back met the wall.

Oliver rested a hand near her head against the wall, looking conflicted. "When I'm frustrated and angry, there's only one thing that helps."

"Which is?"

He feigned a look of discomfort in response to her question. "It'll sound crass if I put it into words."

"I see." Her voice adopted a husky undercurrent. She swallowed, allowing her need to slowly reassert itself as he toyed with the uneven hem of her dress.

"That makes it hard to know what I can do to help." His fingers grazed her bare thigh, causing sensations to radiate from the touch.

Oliver's grin could have appeared welcoming, if only his stare weren't so direct.

"I wouldn't worry about you being confused."

"Okay." The response made her sound every bit the eager little girl. Her heart went to her throat when his gaze lingered on her mouth.

"Wait," she moaned when only a hair's breadth separated their lips. "You said you couldn't have sex in your sister's house." She watched him raise his head a fraction and gave herself a mental kick for ruining the moment.

Oliver grinned, brushing the back of his hand across her cheek. "She'll forgive me."

Chapter 7

Minka's whimper sounded loud just as Oliver's tongue teased her parted lips. His unhurried manner was an aphrodisiac all its own. His hand continued to rest against the wall while the other stayed on her thigh, strong fingers outlining lazy circles along the satiny inside. His tongue teased her mouth, using the same lazy caresses.

Minka was eager for the kiss that was too slow in coming. Not that the man's teasing wasn't an arousing treat, but she'd been tempted enough by his kisses over the past several days.

Oliver grinned when she snagged his collar—a silent demand that he lower his head. The grin grew more defined as he resisted her tugs and succeeded in making her stand on her toes in an attempt to reach his mouth.

Oliver braced against the wall out of necessity. His

legs had gone almost totally weak. Minka sighed, content as their tongues tangled in a light tentative duel. The kiss transitioned from tentative to thorough within moments.

Minka loosened her hold on Oliver's collar, and she felt the floor give way beneath her feet when he lifted her.

Oliver broke the kiss, groaning deep into Minka's neck. "I don't want to take you against a wall, but you're close to making me do just that."

"What should I do about that?" She trailed her fingers across his nape and over his shoulders before tangling them in his hair.

"Don't worry about it," Oliver said as he gently took her hand.

He found his way to the guest bedroom suite with the surety of a man familiar with his surroundings. Within minutes, Minka felt her back touch the pillow-top decadence of her guest's bed. Oliver studied her there, the stunning stare he possessed raking her from head to toe and back again. Then, he was moving in, hunching over her—his arms and torso creating a potent, sensual cage.

"Are you sure?" he murmured, then skimmed her calf with his lips. "I need to hear you say it, Minka," he urged when she only whimpered obligingly.

"Yes, yes…" Her chant ended on a throaty moan when his mouth reached her inner thigh. "Oliver," she began to tug at the lacy panties hugging her hips.

Oliver captured Minka's wrists and pressed them into the folds of the dress bunched above her waist. The garment's lush folds covered her breasts, the hem tickled at her chin.

The sensation was lost on Minka. Her senses were

more in tune to his skillful mouth grazing the dip of her inner thigh. She arched her back, offering her body in anticipation of him feasting upon the part of her that most craved for the pleasure his mouth promised. His forearm across her belly gave Minka hope that she was on the verge of receiving what she desired.

Oliver hooked a thumb beneath the side stitch of the lacy lingerie. He held it there but did nothing to remove the garment. He increased the pressure of his arm over her stomach when she tried to arch her back once more. She squeezed at the offending arm, then pulled her fingers through her hair when he refused to budge.

Minka shuddered his name when he launched a tormenting nibble at her skin. It was just the slightest movement of his coaxing lips. They eased closer, deliberately seeking until they skimmed the panties' crotch. She squirmed beneath the rush of sensation spiraling through her womb.

Her whimpers and soft words of encouragement did nothing to spur him on. Minka accepted that she'd have to settle for the delicious yet inadequate pleasure gleaned from his touch.

"Oliver, please." She was mad with expectation of having his mouth where she most wanted it. Her hips bucked in earnest, her pleas gaining volume when he kissed her sex, tonguing her folds through the middle of the panties he didn't seem interested in removing.

He didn't seem to mind Minka's wriggling and twisting to free herself of her clothing. But at last, she had worked herself free of the dress's sheer fabric.

Oliver worshipped the rich, chocolaty hue of her skin—even and flawless, it accentuated her curvy proportions. How was it that this woman had enchanted him as completely with her mindset and manner as she had with her body? he wondered.

"Oliver…" Her whimper held the clear tinge of impatience then when she tugged at the tails of the crisp shirt lying outside his trousers. He rose up slightly, aiding in her removal of the shirt. Together they turned and tussled, soft laughter coloring the room as they undressed each other.

Soon, nothing but the satin comforter and sheets lay tousled about their nude bodies. Oliver muttered an obscenity that held all the chords of appraisal. There was something comforting about the way she felt next to him, bare and alive carried a novelty—a rare beauty.

He smiled, nuzzling his face beneath her jaw while trying to accept that he had definitely lost all control over his reason.

Minka moved against him with such a seamless sensuality, it almost stopped his breath. Her bottom nudged his sex as he spooned her, keeping her back flush with his chest by cupping one breast and subjecting the nipple to a merciless round of strokes and squeezes.

Her cries were low and unsteady. She turned her face into a pillow when he exchanged toying with a pebbled nipple for skimming his hand down her torso. His fingertips curved into the faint dusting of curls framing the juncture of her thighs.

"May I?" He murmured against her ear as he nibbled the lobe.

Resistance wasn't even conceived, especially once his middle finger commenced its assault upon her clit. Her cries into the pillow, gained volume while her thighs trembled and provided Oliver with the entrance he requested.

Soft, satisfied rumbles in his chest mingled with her cries when he breached her sex. Moisture coated his fingers, galvanizing his arousal to a sweltering pitch. He needed to be inside her, plundering and exploring the secrets of her body the way his fingers had the honor of doing just then.

"I want this to last, Mink."

She smiled, hearing the ragged element in his tone that seemed to accuse her for foiling his plans. Her delight was evident when he put her on her back and took his own delight in the silken texture of her thighs once he'd settled between them.

He groaned her name as though he'd been newly stricken by the joy their current position allowed. She moaned his name but offered no additional details of what it was she wanted.

Oliver required no clarification. He smoothed out the bedcovers until he fisted the trousers tossed aside earlier. He handled them awkwardly until he'd extracted what he'd been attempting to retrieve from his pockets.

The sultry curve of Minka's mouth grew more defined when she heard the distinct crinkle of the condom's packaging. He ended the suckling kiss he'd given to her earlobe and she whimpered her agitation. The emotion was short-lived when she saw that he'd only broken contact in order to rip open the foil wrapper with his teeth.

Minka took it upon herself to retrieve the wrapper and proceeded to apply their protection. Oliver had made it clear that her intimate touch was a bit more stimulation than he wanted then. Minka took great pleasure in examining his thick length filling her hand as she set the condom in place.

Time wouldn't allow for further exploration, though. Her eyes locked with his when he took possession of her thighs and claimed her body in a swift plunge that forced a throaty gasp from the back of her throat.

They were sheltered amidst the tangle of covers, but Oliver changed that. He freed Minka from the twisted sheets, her bare legs lying atop the covers while he remained shielded beneath them from the waist down. His lean hips moved vigorously back and forth, thrusting with a savage energy as he branded her sex with his.

Minka wrapped her legs high around his back, shuddering out moans that were wrapped in his name as the penetration deepened. Her hands curved into half fists against his chest. She didn't seek to push him away, merely to brace herself to accept every erotic pump that rocked her hips in a devastating sway she wished to fully absorb.

Oliver sheltered his face deep at the dip between her neck and shoulder. He didn't want to deny his sex one second of the pleasure it enjoyed being inside hers—pampered by the sweetly painful squeeze of her intimate muscles.

He feared he'd be coming much sooner than he wanted, especially when her round nails began their rhythmic stroking of his spine. He gave freedom to his restraint, shuddering her name into her skin as waves of his need coated the inside of the condom with repeated sprays of satisfied longing.

Depleted, they worked to slow their rapid, heavy breaths, which, for a while, were the only sounds to fill the room.

* * *

"Mr. Spring, I really do appreciate you working with my schedule."

Calvin Gregory Spring waved a hand and shook his balding head. "Not a problem," he told the man seated on the other side of his desk. "It's not every day someone with your skill shows up in our applicant pool." Apology filled the man's vivid green eyes. "We're only sorry that we can't offer you a more competitive salary, one befitting someone with your level of expertise."

Will Lloyd waved off Spring's words. "I'm thankful to have the job, sir, considering the way I was so abruptly let go from my previous employer."

"Ah, yes." Spring's understanding smile showed signs of tightening, and he shuffled through papers in the folder on his desk.

"These things happen, Lloyd." Spring tapped at something in the folder. "You've stated your reason for dismissal as a difference of opinion."

Will nodded, tugging the cuff of his olive-green jacket while shifting in his chair. "I didn't see eye to eye with one of my supervisors in the handling of certain aspects of Mr. Wilder's charitable foundation. The supervisor had seniority as well as previous experience in the position I held, so…"

Spring nodded in understanding. "I commend you on being so forthright in explaining those circumstances. Most wouldn't be quite so cordial about their former employer, seeing how hard a job is to come by in this economy."

"Well, sir, it was an honor to simply be brought in to Wilder in the first place. Qasim runs a top-notch firm, with top-notch people. I can only hope my experience there has prepared me to be a greater asset to your business."

"I'm sure it will." Spring stood behind his desk. "If you're ready, I'd like to show you around and introduce you to the people you'll be working most closely with in the accounting pool."

"Thank you, sir." Will was already on his feet.

"Aside from the manager over there, no one else on the team holds quite as much financial expertise as you do. Having someone to provide your level of guidance on the allocation of our funds will prove quite beneficial." Spring rounded his desk.

"I agree, sir." Will moved closer, extending his hand for a shake that Spring accepted. "Don't worry, sir. Your money is in good hands."

Sleeping in was something Oliver Bauer was quite familiar with and greatly enjoyed. He believed in playing and relaxing as seriously as he worked. When he woke that morning to find the bedside clock reading 10:12 a.m., he wasn't stunned by the time. He was stunned, though, for he was quite *un*familiar with sleeping in with any woman who had graced his bed the night before.

He never stayed over—never had to deal with women staying over either for he had never put himself in a position of inviting one to his bed. He hadn't broken his second rule of thumb. Yet, he knew that, if given the opportunity, he'd not only invite Minka Gerald to his bed, he would do everything in his power to keep her there.

For more than just one night? Yes. Most definitely, yes.

Last night, for him, had gone beyond his other experiences. He'd never questioned that he would stay the night.

Minka had curled into him trustingly, nuzzling her dark and lovely face into his neck and falling asleep almost instantly. Oliver recalled the way his eyelids had grown heavy from the pressure of exhaustion. The sweet pressure of contentment had coaxed him into the precious depths of sleep.

Now, the first to wake, he lay there propped up on his elbow, watching her. Long brows drew closer as though he were in the midst of solving some mystery.

How had this woman stopped him as no other had? He wanted to solve the riddle of her but would have to be content with just enjoying what she did for him. Perhaps it was the fact that she *was* a riddle, and once it was solved...

Oliver shook his head, not wanting to contemplate what lay beyond. Her breathing pattern had changed, and he noticed her flinch a bit in her sleep.

Minka opened her eyes, frowning as she attempted to focus. She smiled sleepily when Oliver's face sharpened before her eyes.

"What time is it?" She stretched as best she could against his lean frame crowding her.

"I'm pretty sure there's a meeting we're late for."

"I should care." She indulged in another stretch. "But for some reason, I don't."

"I believe Miami is working its black magic on you."

"I believe you're right." Minka laughed then watched his expression more closely. "What?"

Oliver brushed his thumb across her clavicle. "I'm sorry, Mink—what happened at dinner last night—

making you think you'd misjudged me. You were really dead-on about the way I operate."

Her expression grew more astute. "I'm guessing that the way you operate has somehow changed."

He grinned, nodding. "Somewhere along the way it has, and that scares the hell out of me. It was so unexpected."

Minka propped up on her elbow, smiling when his eyes dropped to where the sheet slipped a few inches from her chest. "How unexpected?" she asked.

Oliver tugged up the sheet. "I didn't realize it until I heard what you thought of me."

"And? Was I right?"

"I thought so. Yet I don't want to stop seeing you when we're done here."

"Oliver..." She pushed herself into a sitting position. "I told you that wouldn't be a good idea."

"You told me." He nodded slowly. "But you didn't tell me all of why."

"I don't want us on the outs again."

"Then stop trying to talk me out of this. You won't."

"So my words mean nothing?"

"Oh, they do. But only 'Oliver, I never want to see you again' has a hope in hell of doing the trick."

She opened her mouth to respond, but Oliver leaned in, cupping a hand behind his ear to indicate that he hadn't heard her.

"Case closed," he said as he covered her body with his and settled her back to the bed.

Minka purred, reveling in his touch. Her pulse quickened in expectation of what part of her body he'd touch next.

"Didn't you say we were late for a meeting?" she

teased, laughing when he responded with a purr of his own.

"We're already late." He nuzzled her ear. "May as well make it count."

Their laughter filled the room.

Chapter 8

"Hello? Yeah? No, you got it right… Hello?" Oliver grinned at his sister's obvious surprise when he answered Minka's phone later that morning. "Vecs? You there?" Laughter held thickly to his every word.

"What are you doing, Olive?"

Oliver leaned against the counter, watching Minka at the kitchen island. "What am *I* doing? Well, I've been at it with Minka all night." He laughed even when Minka rushed over to swat at his chest.

"Oliver!" Vectra was screaming through the line. "That is *not* a good idea."

"Calm down, Vecs." Oliver laughed while fending off Minka's blows. "We're down here working on a huge project that's got to be put together in record time, and we had to pull an all-nighter. What'd you think I meant?" His grin turned more devilish, and he hugged Minka to his chest when her blows ceased.

"What are you doing with her phone?" Vectra asked.

Oliver's demeanor changed and Minka couldn't help but notice the transformation. She understood why after his next words to his sister.

"We got our phones mixed up, Vecs. I must've thought it was mine." He studied Minka closely.

"Can I speak to her?" Vectra asked.

"Sure, here she is."

Oliver held the phone just out of Minka's grasp and leaned in close, indicating the price for the phone was a kiss.

Minka obliged, expecting the gesture to be a quick sweet peck. What she got instead was a thorough claiming, as lusty as it was possessive.

"Vectra, hi!" Minka prayed her breezy, sweet manner would prove an effective cover for her arousal.

"Hey girl, how's everything going?"

"It's such a great place, Vectra. Thanks for letting me stay. I have to keep reminding myself that I'm here for work and not play." She swatted at Oliver's hand when he tried to tug the belt free of her robe.

"Well good, good." Vectra sounded completely satisfied...and relieved. "We'll get together for lunch when you get back."

"Sounds good. I want to hear some stories about your getaway with Sim."

"Oh, yes." Vectra laughed. "That getaway took a really exciting turn."

"Oh? Any details to share?"

"Lots but...better if I tell you when I see you."

"Okay." Minka smiled at the playful mystery. "Did you want to talk to Oliver again?"

"Yeah, thanks, Minka. Bye."

"Vecs?" Oliver greeted when he had the phone again.

"Just wanted to remind you of what I said regarding your health."

Oliver chuckled. "I remember it very well. If that's it, I need to be getting back on the grind with Minka." He grinned adorably until his arresting stare settled to Minka and became more heated.

"'Bye," Vectra hastily grumbled and disconnected.

Oliver went to Minka and dropped the phone into her robe pocket. "You don't want to lose that…or do you?"

"What?" She laughed while turning to face him.

"You looked at the thing like it had the plague when it rang before." All traces of play had diminished from his eyes. "Something you'd like to tell me?"

She maintained her playful air. "Maybe taking a call right now isn't ranking high on my list of preferred activities."

"Mmm-hmm…is that 'taking a call' in general, or 'taking a call' from Will Lloyd?"

"Oliver." Minka threw back her head. "You got here during a really awkward moment. Will just showed up. I wasn't expecting to see him here, is all."

Oliver looked ready to argue that, but he didn't. "I should hit the road and slap on a change of clothes."

"Ah yes, for the meeting we missed."

He met her tease with a quick smile. "Sorry for not being better prepared. I'm not used to staying the night."

Minka nodded, hugging herself as she shrugged. "I hope it was a nice change of pace."

"I could be persuaded to show you how nice a change it was."

Smiling, she stood on her toes and kissed his cheek. "See you later."

Oliver eased an arm about her waist a second after her lips brushed his jaw. He released her after almost a minute and said nothing more as he left the kitchen.

Minka only watched, not making a move until she heard the front door close. "Careful, Minka." She expelled the advice on a sigh. Men like Oliver Bauer were made to fall in love with.

She heard her phone chime in with another call. Minka ordered herself to answer and was pleased to find her grandmother on the other end of the line.

"So when are you coming home?"

"Well, what's the rush?" Minka laughed.

"Mmm, no rush. Just thought I might try to change your mind about all this."

"Hmph, and I might let you," Minka replied without thinking. Her gaze drifted toward the doorway Oliver had just walked out of.

"Is that right?" Something in the way her granddaughter voiced the sentence apparently sparked Zena's romantic notions. "Have you met a boy, Mi-Mi?"

Minka had to laugh over the way Zena phrased the question.

"No, Gram Z., I haven't, I'm just…just enjoying the good life I so seldom get to enjoy."

"Well, my love, you'll definitely have time for that once you claim your place at BGI. You'll be amazed by all the party invites that will shower down like a monsoon! You're about to become a true jet-setter, Baby-love."

Minka smiled forlornly. "That doesn't leave much time for those…more important things you've been telling me to give a chance."

"Well…one thing doesn't mean the other is off-limits, you know?"

Minka leaned against the kitchen island, delighting in the wordplay with her grandmother. "Tell me how you know that? *Your* one thing and your work pretty much went hand in hand."

"True…but Minka, trust me, you'll know the man when you meet him. You'll see him for what he is the same way that he'll see you for what *you* are."

"Right. And what happens when he sees what I have, like other—"

"Shush, Mi-Mi. The others don't matter, you hear me? I don't want to see you grow into one of those bitter women, always comparing each new man to the old weasels that betrayed them."

"It's a valid point, Gram."

"Perhaps." Zena gave an indignant sniff. "Perhaps. But try not to focus so intently on *that point* that you lose sight of a man who won't even give it a second thought, hmm?"

"How'd you get so wise?"

Zena burst into laughter. "Ah, honey chile, I could tell you some stories."

"Really?" Minka faked an amazed tone of voice. "I thought I'd already heard them all."

"Hardly! We'll plan a story session when you get back."

Minka giggled. "I look forward to it."

"Well, then I'll let you get on with your day, Baby-love."

"All right, Gram. I love you."

"I love you too, sweetness."

Minka studied the phone once the call ended. *Don't*

compare a new man with an old weasel. Funny and true, but how realistic was it? Who she was…the money…it all inevitably became an issue.

Her phone launched into another round of ringing.

"This is Minka." She left the island to carry empty coffee mugs to the sink. She was about to start rinsing them when she realized the caller hadn't spoken. Instead of wasting time with another *hello*, she shut off the call and made another.

"Hey, hey, hey, Mini-Mink!" The man who picked up the other end of the line had a gregarious tone and hearty laughter that practically enveloped his words.

Minka couldn't resist laughing along with him. "Hey, Mr. Walt."

Walter Penner's contagious humor could set anyone at ease. He and Minka made small talk for a while. She asked about his family, including his seven grandkids. Walt asked about Zena, whom he hadn't seen in a few months.

"So have you taken the top spot yet, little girl?"

"Soon, Mr. Walt."

"I tell ya… Bry would be some kind of proud to have you in his chair, honey."

Minka felt a rush of appreciation. Coming from Walt, that meant a lot. Walter Penner had been friends with Bryant Gerald long before Bryant began to build his company.

Walter, a burly, outwardly intimidating man, possessed the gentlest of souls. He had served as the buffer between Bryant Gerald and the world that had scoffed at a black man who thought he could become an entrepreneur, and a successful one at that. Minka knew that Walter Penner had been her grandfather's most trusted friend.

"Mr. Walt, I need a favor, and please wait until you hear all the particulars before you agree. Um…you can't speak about any of this with my grandmother."

"Minka…" he growled.

"Mr. Walt, I have to ask this. Gram Z. would worry if she knew, and I'm sure there's no need."

"Uh-huh, yet you're not quite convinced, or else you wouldn't be asking me to keep quiet."

She winced, bracing herself to continue. "I, uh, I need to have a number traced."

Walter's growl rumbled. "What in Hades have you gotten yourself into?"

"I'm fine, I'm fine. I promise I'm not in any kind of danger." Minka paced the kitchen. "I'm just getting some calls that have me a little concerned."

"Hang-ups?"

"Not exactly. Uh…the person calls and stays on the line without saying anything. Do you think you could put some kind of trace on the calls to see where the weird ones are coming from?"

"Of course I can," Walt replied as though the request were child's play. "Are you calling from the phone now?"

"Mmm-hmm." Minka heard the man softly reciting numbers on the other end and guessed he was copying her number from the caller ID.

"All right, so…is there anything else I'm not supposed to do?"

"That's it."

"Ha! That's enough, Miss Mink. Zena will skin me alive if she finds out about this."

"Thanks anyway, Mr. Walt."

"Yeah, yeah." Walter faked his gruffness. "Do you need protection, girl? I can send some guys out to watch over you."

"Oh no, no, I don't think all that's necessary."

"How about lettin' me provide you with a gun?"

Minka took time to carefully consider the offer. "I think I'll be okay. Uh, how long do you think it'll take to get the trace?"

"Shouldn't be long at all. I'll call when I've got something."

Minka nodded. "Thanks, Mr. Walt." She waited for Walter to disconnect before she did the same. Smoothing a hand across her jaw, she scanned the empty kitchen beneath a guarded gaze. "What are you up to, Will?"

The fact that men outnumbered women on the Austin Sharpe trip hadn't gone unnoticed by Oliver or by any of the other men.

The events almost seemed to be planning themselves, which put everyone at ease enough to viciously tease Austin about the male-to-female ratio.

Austin was laughing heartily while refilling his drink at the well-stocked cart that had been placed on the terrace for the early lunch with his senior execs and Oliver's team. Talk of business had lasted until halfway through lunch, then conversation had turned to more entertaining topics such as sports, music…and women.

On the subject of women, Oliver wasn't surprised to hear Minka's name mentioned more than once. Unfortunately *once* was one time too many for him. When one of the men asked Austin to saddle him with a few responsibilities that might get him closer to Minka, Oliver shared that she didn't date guys she had a business relationship with. When the guy celebrated that fact and told Austin to forget the extra responsibilities, Oliver muttered a curse under his breath.

"Hey, Austin? Do you know if she dates white guys?"

"Are we done?" Oliver asked before Austin could answer.

"All right, guys," Austin said. "Meeting adjourned." He made his way to the bar. "Looks like Ms. Gerald's made an exception to that rule of hers about not dating guys she does business with," he sang when Oliver approached.

"Her rule hasn't been broken." Oliver finished prepping a glass of bourbon. "Just slightly trampled."

"Slightly trampled, huh?" Austin chuckled. "Enough for you to already be laying claim to the woman?"

"Hell." Oliver winced and downed the drink. "You think anybody noticed?"

"Don't worry about it." Austin shrugged. "They can be a little slow on the come-up, especially with a beauty like Minka blinding them to everything else." He clapped Oliver's shoulder. "I'm sure they'll all get the picture after tomorrow night's get-together, especially if you wear your heart on your sleeve like you did today at lunch."

"She'd kill me," Oliver grumbled as if to himself.

"Dammit man, I'm impressed." Austin leaned back to regard Oliver curiously. "You really care about her, don't you?"

Oliver offered no response.

"I get it," Austin said. "Minka's more than a beauty— she's smart and has a business mind few can match."

"It's obvious that Sim taught her well," Oliver said.

"Perhaps." Austin finished his vodka and water, and took it back to the table. "You know I've been around folks who've been *taught* the business, and I've been around ones who *live* the business.

"There's a seamlessness." Austin sighed while re-claiming his seat at the table. "Like they aren't out to prove the same things that the rest of us are." He shrugged. "Didn't mean to wax philosophical, it's just an observation. Whatever it is, Minka's got it. So do you and I, but she's definitely got it."

Oliver realized then how little he knew about the woman he'd made love with less than twelve hours ago. And they had *made love*—he refused to accept it as anything less. At any rate, he *didn't* know her, and that needed to change.

Chapter 9

Minka showered and changed into what would become her attire for the day. The risqué white string bikini had a bottom that consisted of two triangular scraps of material meant to cover her ample bottom. She eyed the garment with high skepticism. The top was also two triangles, which covered her nipples and not much else.

Minka took one look at herself in the mirror, loving everything she saw. She'd never have worn the piece to a public pool or beach. She wondered if she'd even wear it for another living soul. Oliver, maybe? She smiled while biting on her thumbnail as his captivating image came to mind. He'd already seen the parts of her that were covered by the scraps of fabric.

Oliver Bauer had taken an almost total possession of her body in the span of a night, and she'd practically begged him for it. She had no regrets. She also had no plans to continue after Miami.

She'd *had* no plans… Had things changed? *No, Minka*, she chided herself. It was obvious that the last thing Oliver Bauer needed in his life was another woman. No matter what his sweet words hinted at or professed. A long-lasting relationship was surely not in his future. Given the kind of social life he had, he'd be a fool to bring himself the agitation of trying to be true to one woman. Still…his words that night had rung with such sincerity.

She gave herself another stronger shake as though that effort was sure to rid her of the man's disturbingly appealing image.

Clearing her throat, Minka straightened on her chaise and tried to focus on the portfolio of work she'd brought down with her to the pool. When her cell phone rang, she didn't take offense to the intrusion.

She read the name on the display as a curious frown tugged her brows.

"Mr. Walt? No way are you *that* good."

Walt Penner released a brash sound akin to laughter. "Little girl, little girl, the stories I could tell you!"

"Oh, I'm sure." She laughed as well. "So how long will you keep me in suspense?"

"Well, I'll tell you, you might think the suspense far more interesting than what I found."

"So you found nothing?"

"Not unless you call a hotel in Salinas something."

"Well, did the call come from a specific room in that hotel?"

"Lil girl…now I told you the suspense was more interesting than the real deal, didn't I?"

"Yeah…yeah you did." A hotel *room* at least had the potential to be connected to a hotel guest, specifically Will Lloyd. Minka thought if she could tie him to the calls, that'd be tangible proof of…something. It'd be a beginning that, with any luck, might show Will Lloyd the inside of a jail cell. Which was where Qasim should've sent him, instead of just letting him off with a slap on the wrist.

"Are you ready to tell me what in blazes that was all about?"

"Mr. Walt, did all the calls come from that hotel?" Minka asked instead.

Walt sighed. "All but one, and I couldn't get a lead on the number, which most likely means a disposable cell."

Minka nodded, disappointed. "Thanks, Mr. Walt. I'm sorry for sending you on a wild goose chase and for not being able to tell you more."

"You just be careful, you hear? And if I have cause to suspect anyone truly sinister following you around, I'm goin' straight to Z. Understood?"

"Understood." Minka heard the click of Walter's phone line. She resumed her study of the portfolio and discovered that although work was a poor distraction from the likes of Oliver Bauer, it was a superb one for the likes of Will Lloyd.

"Minka?"

Oliver arrived at the condo later that afternoon. He'd knocked and waited almost a minute at the front door before he grew impatient and headed around back. He'd noticed the car she'd rented parked along the street. She was there, just not answering the door or…perhaps out. He wondered if the hypothetical outing was business or pleasure, and the thought only fueled his need to investigate until he had a solid answer.

"Mink?" He'd gone around back and heard her laughing.

The high gate shielding the pool area was unlocked, and Oliver grimaced, agitated with himself for not making sure that it was secure during his last visit. He heard Minka laugh again, forgot his agitation and eased the door open. He followed the palm-lined walkway that zigzagged along the shaded patio and discovered that she was on the phone.

Oliver couldn't have been more pleased when he saw Minka standing from the lounge. She missed his arrival, thereby giving him the opportunity to observe her unaware.

Minka was in the throes of laughter and thoroughly enjoying her phone conversation. Some of the possessiveness in his inspiring eyes made room for softness when he realized she was talking to her grandmother. The easy singsong manner of her voice stopped him somehow. Her tone was patient yet carefree, with a loving reverence for the woman.

His gaze fixated on the tiny pieces of material that served as her bikini. His need to touch her, to feel her on his skin, was so intense that the nerve endings tingled in his palms.

Oliver slowly followed her into the house to make good on his desire. Her responses to her grandmother were wider spaced, softer, as though the conversation were winding down.

Minka had strolled through the house, oblivious to the man following her through the vast condo. She'd ended the call with Zena by the time she returned to her bedroom. With one hand cupped near the bikini strings tied at her hip, she used the other to massage the small of her back. She cast a longing look toward the bed.

"To hell with it," she muttered, climbing onto the bed and crawling to the middle. Then she saw Oliver, and everything went still for a moment.

Minka eased down to rest her bottom on her calves, where they were bent beneath her. "I didn't expect you back—" She curbed the sentence, spotting the signs of his temper. It was well-restrained temper, but temper all the same rising in his eyes. "I expected Austin's meeting to go on for at least five more hours."

"Fortunately, it didn't, or I would've missed...all this." His gaze coasted over her thighs and back to her face.

She shrugged faintly. "But you've already seen it."

He smiled. "And you thought once was enough?" He sounded both curious and amused.

She gave another shrug. "Isn't it usually?"

"You're not my usual."

"Oliver...are you trying to tell me I'm different?" she teased.

Oliver seemed to be turning the word over in his mind. "Different...you are." He moved to the bed, took his time scanning her body again and said, "But in more ways than the one currently running through your head."

"And you believe all those ways are going to keep you occupied for the rest of our trip, and beyond it?"

"Minka, Minka...so suspicious of my motives. Isn't my word good enough?"

"Sure." Her smile reciprocated his cunning. "You're very good with your words."

"I'm good with all sorts of things. Or have you forgotten already?"

"Hmm..." It was Minka's turn to appraise him beneath a dark, brilliant stare. "It's kind of a blur."

"That's a shame. What can we do about that?"

"Not sure." She made another appreciative survey of him in his navy carpenter's pants and a white cotton shirt rolled at the sleeves. "You're not exactly dressed for what would be appropriate here."

"I'm not..." He leaned over, trapping her beneath him. "But you are," he whispered near her temple.

It took no time at all to free one of her breasts from the bikini top. He worked the nipple around his tongue and between his perfect teeth until the bud pebbled. Minka responded to the sensation with a weak moan. That moan turned into a whimper when his hand moved to wedge between the deep valley of her breasts, down to her torso. There, he circled her navel with the tip of an index finger until she fidgeted, gripping his wrist and directing his hand to a more preferable locale.

"I really came here to give you an update on the meeting," he said.

"But why?" Her voice was a purr as she eased his hand inside the triangular front of the bikini bottom. "You do this so well."

Her comment, meant only to tease, gave Oliver pause. But then his fingertips were grazing her welcoming folds. When she smiled her satisfaction, relaxed back into the bed and spoke his name in the softest pleading manner, she also dissolved any lingering hesitation. Only faintly then did her eagerness and acceptance for their relationship to be about sex and nothing more nag at something inside him.

Minka bit down on her lip, arching her body when he tended her sex with faint up and down strokes that transitioned into a plundering of her sex. She was moist and instantly ready for him.

Oliver's insatiable desire demanded gratification. But for once, his gratification was about her pleasure.

Minka was tumbling into a sweet abyss comprised only of her desire for the man who explored her body with such rapt attentiveness that she felt sustained by it. She smoothed her hands across the bed, indulging in the feel of the cool, crisp sheets against her skin. The sensations contrasted beautifully against the sultry intimate heat he stoked where his fingers claimed her.

Oliver's smile was a mingling of pleasure and possessiveness as he watched her losing herself in a tidal wave of arousal. Her hips rolled, moving in a decadent rhythm of beautiful hunger while she took his fingers, two, then three inside. He was so in tune to her reaction, in tune to the way her inner muscles clenched and squeezed his fingers as she bathed them in a flood of need. He was captivated by her dark and lovely face— his expression was one of elation and desperation.

"No… Oliver, please." Minka squeezed his wrist when she felt him withdrawing. Her moan was one of disappointment when he overpowered her restraint and made good on his threat of retreat. She turned her face into a pillow and attempted to quell her body's cravings. Her breathing spiraled out of control.

Her hips continued to arch and circle on the memory of his touch. She called his name as though he were torturing her. Then she felt the ties loosening at her hip bones.

The bed dipped beneath Oliver's weight as he shifted

upon it. Minka turned from the pillow, smiling with a hopeful curiosity when she saw his face so close to hers. Gently, she stroked his jaw, marveling in its flawless appeal. Her expression was alight with more intense curiosity when he shifted again, moving down her body with a predatory stare.

He settled between her thighs, the material of his shirt grazing her bare skin. Minka arched off the bed when the tip of his nose traced the tops of her thighs before giving her sex its greatest attention. Her hands shot up, her fingers threading through the chestnut-brown curls crowning his head. She had but a moment to luxuriate in their uncommon silken texture before Oliver was securing her wrists to the bed, one at either side of her waist.

His nose rotated the sensitized batch of nerves at her center, causing her entire body to seize in mindless pleasure. She braced against his hands, but it wasn't her freedom she sought.

"Oliver..." She moaned her pleasure when he submitted to her. His tongue was soothing, a warm massage upon her folds. He explored her silken crevices at length and then took her with a sudden thrust as she peaked. She cried her enjoyment with no shame, filling the room with sound.

Oliver cupped her hips in an unrelenting hold meant to still the robust stirrings of her hips. His tongue lunged deliberately, but with a surety that proved he was well aware of how far he was taking her, how close she was to coming apart on him.

With her hips imprisoned, Minka expressed her frustration as well as her delight in the way her body was being treated. Intermittently, she beat her fist to the tangled covers and curled her fists into the crisp material. Her thighs trembled furiously, her back arching while the pressure of release grew heavy at her sex. The dazed and breathless way she called Oliver's name did nothing to attract his attention. Her lids felt heavy, but she could see his head moving tirelessly between her thighs. He feasted as though what he found at her core was in some way nourishing.

Oliver moaned out words of satisfaction. He took pleasure in the pleasure he gave to Minka. There was something else at work there, however. While the giving of pleasure was indeed satisfying, he had never experienced gratification while orally stimulating a woman. Yet, there he was. His dick was swollen, throbbing and promising release within a few more moments of having his tongue so erotically squeezed.

Their mingled breathing was shattered by the effects of the climax laying claim to them both. Oliver kept Minka's hips in a grip that was firm but not bruising. His shoulders were broad, powerful enough to keep her quaking thighs spread to his preference. Minka opened her mouth to share another moan with the room, but no sound emerged. She threaded her fingers into his hair again and was immediately taken over by the nudging his head made against her palms as he so steadily moved.

Sharper cries ricocheted through the air then, and they both labored beneath the weight of an immense satisfaction. Oliver's hands glided up over her torso until they closed over her breasts, partly covered by the triangular swatches of cloth of her bikini top. Her tremors were beginning to cool, as were Oliver's.

He needed a bit more willpower to cool what raged

in his bones, however. Minka tugged at his shirt, and he accepted her invitation to kiss.

Minka treasured the act. Her body on his mouth was a treat she wanted to savor without end. But something told her she wouldn't get that chance. Too soon, he was brushing her cheek with his thumb and giving her a resigned look that said his mind was on more than their mutual pleasure.

"I should let you get back to what you were doing," he said.

Her smile was a wicked one. "So get undressed, then."

Smiling, he let out a soft rush of breath. "I didn't mean to take advantage of you...following you through the house and...having my way with you." He winked.

"Would you have a problem with me telling you that I like the way you take advantage?" she sighed.

"As long as you don't have a problem with me saying that I did as well."

"Well..." She sang the word while scooting up in bed. "It's why we're here."

"Right—to have fun." He bowed his head, feeling a jaw muscle clench from rising tension. "In Miami."

"Ol—"

"No, it's okay, I'm sorry." He cupped her face, putting a kiss to the corner of her eye. "I'll see you later."

Minka watched the doorway long after he'd gone.

Chapter 10

Miami houses were a study in excess. Austin Sharpe's place in the coveted Star Island area of South Beach took that truth to another level. The fifty-thousand-square-foot Spanish colonial villa flickered like a gem against the backdrop of the Atlantic.

Minka put on her happiest face when she arrived that evening, even though she wasn't exactly sure what to expect. She hadn't spoken to Oliver alone since he'd left the condo yesterday. She'd wanted to call and had picked up the phone many times to do that very thing, but she'd made herself be patient.

She shook off the memory of what she'd seen in his eyes when he left, and then observed the party with a hopeful gaze. There were only a few people she knew, as she hadn't been introduced to Austin's full staff since they had arrived.

Smoothing her hands over her hips, which were snug in brick-red slacks, Minka headed in. She introduced herself to those who were unfamiliar.

Austin found Minka by the time she was engaged in her second conversation of the evening. "Gunther! I see you've met our brain trust." He sent a flourishing wave in Minka's direction.

"I have." Gunther Dubose favored Minka with a smile that was without a doubt flattering. He surveyed her curves in a manner that wasn't overtly lecherous, but obvious nonetheless.

"I wonder if you could excuse us for a second, Gun?"

"Right now?" he blurted.

Austin was already leading Minka away. "You won't even miss her," he told his VP of Research and Development.

"Austin—"

"Trust me, Gun, when I say this is for your own good."

"What was that about?" Minka asked when they were away from the frowning VP.

"Oliver's here."

Minka's heart attempted an awkward flip inside her chest. "Does he need to talk to me?"

"Not right now. He's talking to his team."

Minka quietly considered the information. "So... what's the urgency?"

"Urgency?" Austin's thick wheat-blond brows drew close, a look of cool realization crossing his face. "He just doesn't want you talking to Gunther, is all."

Minka stopped midstep. "Are you serious?"

Austin shrugged, and Minka could only shake her

head at the ease with which men staked claims. Instead of feeling angry or outraged, she felt like laughing.

"I'm sorry he's making you babysit."

"Ah, happy to do it. It's rare to see a guy like Oliver Bauer lose all that smooth swagger of his over a woman."

"Rare?"

Austin winced, apparently not agreeing with the word either. "It's almost nonexistent."

"Should I be concerned?" She knew she had no reason to be, but was curious to hear Austin's take on her lover.

"You only have reason to be concerned if you don't wish to be pursued."

Minka inclined her head in a flirtatious manner. "Being pursued isn't so bad, and from what I've heard, Oliver does it very well."

"But to hear him talk, Minka, you've not only attracted him, you've got his full attention."

Her dark eyes narrowed. "What's the difference?"

"Can I speak frankly?"

"Haven't you been?"

Austin took a few seconds to chuckle. "I've known Oli a long time. It's a thing of beauty to see him charm a woman, but now, this is an Oliver Bauer I don't know. He's questioning the potency of that charm, second-guessing everything he does when it comes to you. The only thing he seems sure of is that he wants to please you. Unless it's about business, he doesn't want you within sniffing distance of another man."

"Did he say that?" She sounded stunned.

"Told you he wasn't acting like himself."

"Where is he?"

"Meeting with his crew out on the veranda."

"Thanks." She squeezed Austin's arm and set out.

Minka waited at the entryway of the veranda. She stood just inside and watched Oliver shaking hands with a few members of his design crew. Their gazes locked, but he didn't urge her to join him once the last crew member had headed off to rejoin the party. Instead, Oliver left the area to take the steps down that led to the shore.

Undaunted, Minka followed after slipping off her heels. Oliver charted a path away from the house, not stopping until they were ensconced in more moonlight than lamplight. The liveliness of the party was only a distant roar.

"Oliver?"

Oliver scarcely tilted his head in response to Minka's call. He faced the ocean, watching the energetic waves crash determinedly against the shore.

"So I guess I wasn't just imagining that you were upset with me when you left yesterday?"

He turned his head then. "You thought that?" His voice carried over the tussling waves.

She moved closer then. "It was pretty obvious, Oliver."

"Yeah, I guess…" He gave a quick shake of his head. "I don't know if I'm coming or going lately."

Minka gave a puny shrug. "Sorry."

"Why?" He turned to her then. "You haven't done anything. Hmph…actually you have."

Minka looked playfully uncertain. "Is *this* where I'm supposed to say that I'm sorry?" She smiled when he laughed.

"You never have to apologize to me, Minka. If anything, I should be thanking you."

Curious, Minka moved to one of two deck chairs set a few feet away on the private strip of beach.

"Thanking me, huh? I hope you plan on explaining that."

Oliver wore a small path in the sand. "My parents... they were crazy in love with each other. My dad almost lost his mind when my mom passed. I had to witness the scariest aspects of that. I had to prep myself to take my dad's place sooner than I was ready, since we didn't know if he would ever be able to function again." He dug his fingers into the bunched muscles at his neck while he spoke.

"I was happy to be there for my dad, but I hated seeing him that way and knowing it was all about love... the loss of it...it made me never want to put myself in a position of having to experience that."

"You're not a hermit, Oliver. Any man with a social life puts himself at risk of falling in love."

Oliver was sure Minka couldn't see his expression in the moonlight.

"I can see you don't know a lot about the way men operate," he said.

"I know enough."

"Then you should know how greedy we are. We take what we want, and we give only what's necessary to ensure we keep getting what we want," he explained. "Our lists of wants are quite short, but I can assure you, Ms. Gerald, that love doesn't usually make the cut. Not until we want it to."

"Like I said..." Minka sighed, smoothing her hands

over the chiffon sleeves of her gold blouse. "A social life does put one at risk for love."

"It's not my social life that's done that." He paced slowly before the chairs. "It's watching Vectra's face light up when she talks about Sim." He shook his head briefly as he grinned. "The girl even lights up when she talks about how *bad* things are going with Sim." He joined in when Minka laughed.

"It was the same with my dad." Oliver sobered. "It got me curious…"

"Curious?"

Oliver stopped pacing. "*You* have me curious."

"About…love?" Minka bristled. She heard a gushing undertone to the word. She couldn't help it. She was truly stunned by what he seemed to be confessing. "Oliver, you don't even know me. You're basing this on physical—"

"Damn straight I am. It's all I know. Physical is all I know, all I've wanted to know. And then here you come out of the clear damn blue." He sent an airy wave in her direction. "You shattered all that without lifting a finger."

"So, you're curious." Minka slapped her hands to her thighs. "What do you plan to do about it?"

The words were hardly past her lips before Oliver was trampling the distance between them and tugging her against him.

"I want to know you, Minka, and I'm gonna need longer than Miami to do it."

"Oliver—"

He kissed her, smothering what he was sure he didn't want to hear. She moaned, welcoming the act as he was sure she would. Eagerly, she clutched his shirt, sleeves

rolled to reveal powerful forearms the tone of rich cinnamon. The shirt's tails hung outside his loose-fit jeans.

Her fingers crept beneath the shirt's hem to stroke
his bare skin. Her tongue battled furiously with his as
she felt the sleek perfection of the defined muscles shap-
ing his abdomen.

Oliver was helpless to do anything other than com-
ply. As much as he wanted to remain loyal to his willpower, his need for her raged at a far more demanding
level.

Her body was a study in dark, curvaceous beauty,
a treat that he was ill-equipped to deny himself. The
sand beneath his feet seemed an inadequate foundation
given the way she weakened his legs.

She moaned his name and added the tiny, infectious
whimpers that stroked his desire for conquest like nothing he'd ever known. Determination sharpened his features as he took her down to the sand and focused on
getting her out of her clothes.

Moonlight shone upon their bodies. Oliver saw sheer
delight enhancing the loveliness of her round face, and
it satisfied him to know he was pleasing her.

The thick, lengthy fringes of his lashes fluttered
when his fingertips skirted the lacy stitching along the
seam of her panties. The knowledge of what the garment
protected roused a groan from the depths of his chest.
He rested his forehead against her clavicle.

"Oliver…" She bucked her hips to entice him into
doing more than simply admiring her lingerie. Her next
moan was deepened when those exploring fingers of
his slipped past the barrier of fabric.

"Yes…Oliver, there, please there," she begged when
he only stroked her folds and did nothing more.

"Oliver…"

"Reciprocity, Minka…"

As desire-addled as her brain was, Minka heard and comprehended his response.

Oliver raised his head to give her a devilishly charming smirk. "Give me what I want—time beyond Miami…" He spared a glance around their moonlit environment. "And I give you what you want." He barely eased the tip of his middle finger inside her moistened core.

Minka arched, hungry and aching for what little he'd give. "No fair," she gasped.

"Maybe not, but I have a feeling that you won't turn it down."

"Damn you," she moaned.

Oliver's chuckle rose softly as he gave her more of his finger.

"Oliver…"

"Give me what I want?" He pushed the finger home slow and deep, grunting his pleasure at the moisture coating his skin. He smiled against her cheek as she whimpered when he fully withdrew the finger.

"Give me what I want?" He renewed the taunt.

The man's restraint was supernatural, Minka thought. She felt as though she were losing her mind, while he remained cool, ruthless in the seductive torment he was subjecting her to.

"Give me what I want?"

The words murmured next to her ear were followed by a wet suckle to the lobe. She dissolved. "Yes, all right, yes, just please, Oliver." She reached down to squeeze his wrist insistently.

Oliver didn't seem fully satisfied by Minka's answer.

Taking her lobe between his perfect teeth, he clenched the satiny dark flesh just enough to grab her attention. "When people give me their word, I expect them to keep it." He pulled back just slightly to look at her. "Understood?"

"Yes." She nodded quickly and laughed blissfully when he rewarded her with a slow fingering that consisted of only a few thrusts.

"Look at me."

She obliged without hesitation.

"Do you understand me, Minka?"

"Yes, Oliver." The reply held traces of impatience. She was fully committed to the answer, but her ability to maintain eye contact was challenged when he resumed touching her.

Minka was fully prepared and ready to receive her release through the act, but Oliver was in the mood for something far more beneficial to them both. Her eyes flew open when she felt him leave her. She was on the verge of crying his name when she saw that he was stripping out of his shirt.

Greedily, she absorbed the sight of him framed in the moonlight once the garment left his back. He moved, scooping her close in an impressive show of strength as he lifted her to place his shirt beneath her. Her clothes were tossed over one of the beach chairs. Once more, he eased back to study her wearing only a strapless bra and the panties he'd fondled her through. A press from his thumb to the heart shaped bow at the center of the lingerie released the front clasp to free her breasts.

Minka arched in an instant as one nipple was beautifully ravaged by his tongue and perfect teeth. The other endured a seductive assault between his thumb and forefinger. She discovered her hands were too weak even to reach up and get lost in the gorgeous gleam of his curls. She only wanted to absorb what he gave her.

Excessive foreplay however wasn't Oliver's only intention for their time together. Minka felt him leave her a third time, and her mouth went dry when she saw his hands at the waistband of his jeans. She squirmed, rattled by anticipation as he deliberately unbuttoned the fly to gradually reveal the burgundy-and-black-plaid boxers beneath. Eagerly, she reached to touch him, but he brushed aside her hand. He tugged a condom from his back pocket, and Minka watched a couple more packets tumble next to their makeshift pallet in the sand. Her lashes fluttered as a throb stabbed her in anticipation.

Protection secured, Oliver scooped Minka close again, repositioning her on the shirt. He spread her wide to accommodate him and took her in one seamless move that filled and stretched her. The sensation was so exquisite, Minka felt orgasmic after only a few of the long, thick strokes he plied her with.

Softly, he chanted her name, and Minka could feel her moisture building in tandem with the rhythm his impressive erection set inside her body. Her cries were unabashed without thought given to any passersby. The ocean's roar was such that it provided effective cover while the moon doused them beneath its hazy light.

It was a perfect setting, made more perfect by the act fulfilling them both. Minka's cries entwined with Oliver's moans. Minka discovered Oliver not only had remarkable restraint, but stamina as well. She lost track of how long he kept her there on the beach. She wouldn't have cared if it were for an eternity.

* * *

"Did you plan this, Oliver?" Minka asked later when they were cuddled together on one of the oversized beach chairs.

"You mean, tonight, or Miami in general?"

"I mean both."

"Well, let's see…" Oliver kept his gaze hooded as it fixed on some distant point along the starry horizon. "Tonight was definitely planned. I saw you talking to that idiot Gunther Dubose, and I asked Austin to get rid of him while I met with my team."

"Hmph." Minka turned her face into Oliver's chest and gave into a brief giggle. "You'll be pleased to know that Austin took those orders very seriously."

"He's a good guy." Oliver propped his chin to the top of Minka's head. "As for Miami in general…that wasn't exactly planned."

"Really?" She fixed him with a playfully doubting look.

Oliver toyed with the cuff of his shirt, which Minka was wearing since he'd taken her out of the sand to hold her in the chair.

"I knew I wanted to sleep with you since that morning I saw you leaving Vectra's. I only solidified my plan during the Frisco meeting about Austin's project."

"Ha! I'm impressed by your confidence."

"Don't be. It hasn't all gone according to plan, remember?"

"Ah yes…those curiosities of yours."

Oliver didn't seem amused by the teasing current to her words. "I know you think I'm full of it, Minka—I don't blame you. Given my track record, any woman in her right mind would take me for a joke if I suddenly came spouting anything that even hinted at longevity."

"You know, the thing about curiosity is that it has a tendency to fade once it's been satisfied."

"That's true."

The silence that fell following his agreement made Minka feel unsettled.

"So what happens when your curiosity is satisfied?"

"Ah, Minka." Oliver cupped her cheek then smoothed the back of his hand across her jaw. "I don't think you're ready to know what happens."

"Yuck—that bad, huh?"

"It's not bad at all." Oliver laughed. "I just don't think you're ready to hear anything I have to say on the subject of 'us beyond Miami.'"

"What if I was ready to hear it?"

"I don't really see my curiosity about you ever being satisfied." He tugged aside the opening of his shirt to appraise her bare form beneath it. "If the time ever came that it was, it wouldn't matter, considering the fact that being curious about you is just the thing that drew me to you. Who you are, how incredible you are to look at, how incredible you feel when I'm inside you—"

"Oliver—"

"Shh…" He whispered, brushing his thumb across her mouth. "You wanted my answer. I'm giving it to you."

"You're embarrassing me."

"No…you're just not used to hearing a man tell you that you've shut him down, that you've halted everything he thought he knew and was content knowing. The way your mind works…" He nuzzled his face into the top of her head. "It fascinates me, and I haven't even had the chance to ask you half the damn things I want to know. I'm sure my main reason for wanting to ask you anything is because I can't get enough of the way you give me your full attention when you speak. The way your eyes scan my face, like I'm the most interesting person you know."

She gave him an acquiescing smile. "I was raised to believe a good business person gives undivided attention."

A scant grimace marred his features. "Guess that's why it irks me to see you talking with guys I know are using business matters as a way to talk you into bed."

Her laughter carried on the night breeze. "I don't think most men have sex on their minds when they approach me."

"That's because you tend to believe the best in people."

"Well, that's good. Otherwise I wouldn't be sitting here in your lap."

"I would've gotten you here. May've taken a while, but I was motivated."

"Ah, yes." Again, she threw back her head. "Curiosity."

Oliver nodded as though his memory had been refreshed, and he resumed drawing back his shirt from her body. "Curiosity…the thing that drew me to you. All the rest, though…" He eased a hand inside the shirt to cup, fondle and squeeze her breast. He molested the tip using the pad of his index finger, until she moaned.

"All the rest, Minka, is what's got me hooked with no hope for rescue. It's what's got me in love with you, Minka."

Minka didn't know if her moan was in reaction to his manipulation of her nipple, the kiss he gave or the words he'd spoken.

Chapter 11

Voices along the shore cut short the intimacy Oliver and Minka had enjoyed along the deserted strip of beach. Just as well, for Minka felt so dumbfounded by Oliver's confession she could barely speak.

She was of little use when he dressed her. Minka felt as though she had to hold on to him for support as they made the hike back to Austin's place. Her legs felt like running water.

In love... The man didn't waste time. Not *falling in love*—he was in full-blown love. She couldn't have affected him that much already; there was no way. She couldn't believe Oliver Bauer had tumbled that far so fast.

If he were any other man, she may have thought his motivation related to money, but he had no clue who she really was, of that she was sure. He truly believed he was...in love with her.

And was she ready to lie to herself and say she didn't feel the same?

The question had hit Minka while she and Oliver took the steps up to Austin's veranda. Hadn't she been falling steadily beneath the grips of her attraction for him? An attraction that was both physically and emotionally charged?

They'd returned to the veranda, but Oliver didn't lead them back through the party. Minka was relieved—mingling and networking were out of the question then. Silence had settled between them until Oliver escorted her back to her car. She had to assure him more than once that she'd be okay before he let her go. He didn't follow her home.

Now, a new morning had dawned, and Minka stood in the kitchen of Vectra's condo wondering what would happen next.

She watched the coffeepot dispensing fragrant splashes of French roast into the glass carafe and wondered if there was still such a thing as love at first sight. She believed it existed. Her grandparents had been proof of that—proof that had lasted over fifty years.

It had been a happy fifty years, at least the years she'd been old enough to remember. It was nothing for Bryant and Zena Gerald to meet for steamy kisses in the middle of the day. Minka had often witnessed such displays of affection.

Did Oliver really feel that way about her? She had seen sincerity in his eyes when he'd professed it.

Common sense and her own experiences in the game of love told her that there were no guarantees. In the end, it was all about one's willingness to take a chance and to risk heartbreak for all the possibilities love boasted. Would Oliver Bauer break her heart or would he treasure it? How long would she wait before she was ready to find out?

Minka forced her attention to the coffee, but its preparation wasn't nearly enough to keep her mind off Oliver. The phone rang, and she considered the interruption a vast improvement.

She smiled at the name that showed up and put the phone on speaker. "Hey, Mr. Walt."

"Hello, and when are you bringing your little butt back out West?"

Minka laughed. "Mr. Walt, I'm fine, I'm heading back home after our main event. Were you just calling to check on me?"

"Somethin' about our last conversation stuck with me."

"Any details?" Minka absently stirred her coffee.

"It's about the hotel where the two calls came from."

"You found a room?"

"Not exactly, but I did a little digging to find out what else Salinas had besides hotels where deadbeats could make prank phone calls."

"And?"

"It's the headquarters for Spring Holdings."

"I see." Minka stopped stirring her coffee. "Um... am I supposed to go 'oooh' or something?"

"Ha! You're Z's grandkid, all right! Same kind of sass!" Walt laughed heartily. "Spring Holdings is a subsidiary of BGI."

"Gerald Industries? Are you sure?"

"Triple-checked it. You think it means anything?"

"Don't know." Minka set down her mug while considering. "It's doubtful...so, um..." She gave a phony sigh of relief. "Is there anything else exciting in Salinas?" She laughed when Walt did.

"I'll let you know, that is, if you want me to keep digging."

"I don't know, Mr. Walt, I mean, I don't want you to keep spinning your wheels on this. Keeping tabs on my phone should be enough, don't you think?"

"I'll keep those calls on my radar, but you come see me when you get back, you hear?"

"I will. Thanks, Mr. Walt." Minka waited until Walter disconnected and then softly repeated. "Salinas..."

Oliver couldn't help but laugh when his father mimicked him over the phone line. Oscar Bauer had just told his son that it was time to leave paradise and come back to the real world.

"So it sounds like everything's going pretty well out there."

"Thank the crew. They're really on their game, Dad."

"Good to hear, but I know you deserve much of the credit. You're makin' the company more and more your own."

"Well, I'm not in the driver's seat. And I don't want to be yet." Oliver tacked on the added sentiment the way he usually did when his father hinted of passing the reins over to him.

"Your time's coming sooner than you think, kid."

"Dad..." Oliver switched his phone to his other ear while shifting uncomfortably behind the wheel of the SUV he'd parked at the business park site. "You'd tell me if everything wasn't all right, wouldn't you?"

"Come on, kid, you know I've been looking at retirement property. Did you think that was just for a weekend getaway?"

"I'm just not in a hurry to see you go, is all. Besides, the clients all love you."

"Hmph, nice try, but they love you too. All those fresh ideas and unrelenting energy—they're just trying to make me still feel needed."

"Whatever you say, Dad." It was Oliver's turn to chuckle.

"Whatever, huh? So that means I can expect you Monday afternoon?"

"So you really need me to be there."

"I really do. This is a client I should've introduced you to long ago. She and her husband weren't just clients—they were great friends to your mother and me."

The mention of Rose Bauer shifted Oliver's attention completely. "How were you, Dad? Before you found her—before you found Mom?"

"Well..." Oscar sounded surprised by the question, but in an easy way. "Hell, kid, you know what it's like. You have your pick, same as I did...women see the gloss, and you can do no wrong. Then there're ones who come along and see the rough edges and they accept them, and you think one of them could be the one." He sighed.

"Then there comes the one who not only sees and accepts the tarnished edges, but you find yourself wanting her to know all the dark and dingy parts of you that she doesn't see. Next thing you know, you're revealing things about yourself that you'd never tell another living soul. And she either thinks you're crazy or just feeding her a load of bunk to get her out of her clothes."

Oliver winced, wondering if he'd been so transparent to Minka.

"I probably confessed things about myself and the way I felt about Rose way before she was ready to hear them." Oscar shared once his soft laughter had trailed to silence.

"You wanted her to know you, though," Oscar continued. "You're impatient to hear yourself saying the words to her, because you need her to know what she's getting into—the kind of man she's got pursuing her heart. The kind of man who would give his life to save hers."

"You're a lucky man to have known love like that, Dad."

"Nothing lucky about it. I was a blessed man. I pray for both my kids to be blessed that way."

"I hope so too," Oliver confessed.

"Ahh...so that's where this conversation stems from." A smile came through clear in Oscar's words. "Anything I should know?"

"Not really... I'm still at the 'she thinks I'm crazy' stage." Oliver tapped his fingers morosely against the steering wheel.

The admission sent Oscar bursting into laughter. "Now, Oli, have you gone and scared some poor girl out of her mind with talk of love?"

"I think I may have, Dad, and even I know it's way too soon. Last thing in the world I want is to scare her, but I had to tell her how I felt."

"I gotta say this is strange talk comin' from the likes of you, Oli."

"Ha! You're tellin' *me*? I don't know if I'm comin'

or goin', Dad. Feels like the man I know and this…new guy…are playin' tug of war."

"Well, well… What the hell is going on out there?"

"I'm in love, Dad." Oliver nodded once, decisively. "In love. Not lust—I know what lust feels like, and this isn't just that."

"I get it, son. I believe you." Oscar's voice carried a hushed reverence. "I guess the real question is, how will you get *her* to believe you?"

Oliver set his head against the rest. "That part's gonna take time."

"Does she live out there in Miami?"

"Nope, she lives right in San Francisco, but she isn't too keen on seeing me once Miami's done. She, uh… she acts like she's just happy with a fling."

"Oh, boy." Oscar laughed again.

"What?"

"Nothing like payback, is there? You've been happy with exactly that for years, haven't you?"

"Yeah…" Oliver rubbed at the sudden pressure near the bridge of his nose. "Yeah, I have."

"Must be refreshing to find a woman who doesn't expect anything more of you."

"Right, refreshing…" Oliver felt his jaw clench.

"So, uh, how realistic will it be for you to make that lunch meeting?" Oscar decided not to press his son for more love life–related details.

Oliver needed only a moment to set his thoughts to less emotional topics. "It should work. I'll call you when I land. Is there anything more I need to know to prepare?"

"Not really—it's more of a social thing, so just bring yourself."

"Got it."

"All right, then, you take care, and I'll see you Monday."

"Sure thing." Oliver opened the driver's side door. "And Dad?"

"Yeah, son?"

Oliver smiled. "Thanks."

Salinas, California

CG Spring was frowning murderously over a stack of papers when his newest employee walked into his office. Despite his frustration, Spring graced Will Lloyd with a broad smile tinged with obvious hope.

"Will, thanks for getting here so fast."

"They told me you needed to see me, sir."

"Yes, yes." Spring gave a weary nod, cast another glance toward the paperwork on his desk. "I've been working with my executive staff trying to decide on a new employee insurance plan, but we don't want to choose any company without first being sure of its stability." Spring shot Will another hopeful look. "I knew you honed your skills at vetting companies while working for Wilder. I hope you won't mind sharing a bit of that knowledge with us?"

"Qasim was a good teacher, sir. He has a true gift for recognizing corporate stability but...I was an apt pupil." Will grinned when Spring clapped and clenched a fist as if that were the news he wanted to hear. "I picked up a bit of that know-how during my time there."

Some of Will's confidence began to wane nevertheless. "Sir, apt pupil or not, this isn't exactly my niche. I'm more suited to dealing directly with employees."

"Which is why I think we found a good fit for you in HR." Spring settled back in his desk chair. "What's needed here is more along the lines of analyzing. It will directly benefit the company's most important assets—its employees. Given that your expertise is in both realms..."

"I'll be happy to help however I can, sir."

Spring nodded, satisfied. "We're trying to decide between three companies—we're basing that decision on how comparable they are to employee salaries, current insurance rates, et cetera."

"Hard to find all of that in one company," Will cautioned.

"Right you are. We're willing to settle for one that hits close and won't gouge our workers like our current insurance monster." Spring motioned to the papers before him. "So far the three in hand are in the lead, surpassing the others we've gone through. We decided to make the final cut based on the overall performance of the companies. Unfortunately, every exec has their own preference. We're hoping fresh eyes and ears might get us looking at this thing more critically."

Will watched Spring gather the paperwork into folders, which the man pushed across the desk to him.

"This is all the outlook information on the companies in question as well as all employee payroll allotments for insurance, retirement—pretty much anything we take money out of their checks for. Chances are you won't need half this stuff, but just in case.

"I've already spoken to Terry." Spring referred to his Director of HR. "She's okay with sharing you with us on this so long as we agree to give you back fast."

"I'll do my best, sir." Will chuckled.

"I have no doubt about that." Spring stood, extending a hand. "Sorry for keeping you so long. Thanks again and let us know if there's anything else you need."

Will shook hands with his boss and then left the office.

"Are you sure? It's not a problem, you know?" Oliver could almost feel the muscles cartwheeling along his jaw. Minka had just told him she'd drive herself to the Gallery V event that evening.

"I've got some stuff to handle for the trip back home, so..."

Don't rush her, Oli. The response sent his jaw muscles into a more frantic dance. Oliver made an intense effort to keep his voice level. "When are you going back?"

"Right after the gallery event."

Oliver pulled the phone from his ear and glared at the device with intentions of crushing it. "What's the rush?" he asked back into the phone.

"There's a meeting I need to get back for," she said.

"Understood."

"How soon after the party will you leave?"

"I was planning to go from the gallery to the airport. It's why I want to drive myself."

"Oh? I thought it was because you didn't want anyone to see us arriving together."

"Oliver..."

"When's your meeting?"

"Monday afternoon."

"So what's the rush?"

Her laughter rose softly. "Is it against the rules to take a day off before going back to work?"

Oliver was quiet for a long moment. "Am I at least allowed to talk to you during the party?"

"Ol—"

"It's all right, Minka, I get it. Talk to you later, okay?"

Minka studied her cell phone when the dial tone sounded. She didn't take offense to the way the call ended. It wasn't her intention to be difficult. She really did need a few hours to breathe before jumping into the family business, not to mention wrapping up her lingering responsibilities at Wilder.

She ignored the quiet all-knowing voice in the back of her mind. The voice accused her of being unfair. Oliver was at least a little right. She *didn't* want their relationship on everyone's lips. She didn't want their West Coast colleagues to know about them.

"Stop." She shook her head and focused on the next call she needed to make. The line connected after one ring, and the full-bodied voice on the other end gave her an amused jolt.

"Lorna Spikes." The woman's tone was demanding and impatient.

"Dial back on the coffee, okay?"

The woman laughed. "Hey, Mink." Suddenly, she cleared her throat in phony formality. "I'm sorry, *Ms.* Gerald."

Lorna's husky tone forced a laugh from Minka. "What the hell is that about, idiot?"

"Oh, come off it, Mink. Word is that Miss Z. is about to make some huge announcement involving her *baby-girl.*"

"That woman…" Minka's sigh was one of playful

agitation. She relaxed back onto the bed where she'd worked from for the past ninety minutes. "I haven't even given notice to Qasim yet."

"Ooooh! Is it true, then?"

"True enough."

"Minka…"

"I know…" Minka read much in the woman's response.

"I mean, for real, Mink. Do you realize you're about to be one of the wealthiest women in the country? Hell, in the *world*?"

Minka snorted out a quiet, amused sigh. "I've always been one of the wealthiest women in the world."

"And now you've got the power to go with it."

"Yeah…"

"Lotta pressure…"

"Hmph, yeah…" Minka studied the ceiling, her gaze woeful.

"Miss Z. still on you about giving her a great-grand?"

"Always."

"And…? Any potential donors to the cause…? No, right?"

Minka didn't bother to spurn the assumption. Her old college roommate knew better than anyone the challenges she'd faced in her search for true love.

"You know, in spite of how easy Miss Z. makes it look, I'm sure being the head of BGI is no cakewalk." Lorna waited a few beats. "Have you thought about what this will do to your social life?"

"Social life… You know, somehow I don't anticipate that being a problem."

"I suppose that's a good outlook. The right one usually shows up when you're not looking."

"So they say…" Minka rolled to her stomach. "So about why I called…"

"Well, wasn't it to request my pledge of allegiance once you obtain the keys to the kingdom?"

"Not just yet, but um…my request *is* work related."

"Ah…in my capacity as Human Resources Guru Extraordinaire?"

"I prefer Chief Director of Acquisitions." Minka gave her friend's proper title.

"Tell me more," Lorna urged.

Minka thumped her fist against a pillow, then reached for the pad she'd mulled over since speaking with Walter Penner. "There's a BGI subsidiary in Salinas, California. I need information on it."

"Acquisitions information." Lorna's tone of finality needed no response. "Are we looking for anything special?"

"Yeah." Minka looked to the pad again. "Yes, we are."

Chapter 12

The Gallery V event carried all the pomp of a Hollywood movie premiere. The expansive stainless-steel building was surrounded by photographers and reporters, who were staking out the red carpet in hopes of getting comments from the guests.

Inside, walls and ceilings appeared to mesh in a joining of glass and rich hardwoods. Showpieces were displayed in wood-grained boxes and illuminated by back lighting, making each piece seem like it was levitating. It was a well-attended affair. Sharpe executives and clients filed into the striking facility after their walk up the red carpet.

Minka sought out members of the Gallery V staff within moments of her arrival. Vectra's Miami team was undoubtedly thrilled by the finished result, and their excitement was definitely contagious.

However, the buzz of excitement didn't take Minka's mind from Oliver for a second. Before searching out members of the Gallery V management team, she'd peeked around to see if she could spot him. She wasn't surprised to find him in a crowd of females.

Minka surveyed the scene with a keen and surprisingly amused gaze. She was too far away to hear what he was saying, but figured it had to be something of high interest given the rapt expressions of the women. What man in his right mind would let that kind of power go to waste?

He actually believed he was ready to turn his back on that—that he was in love with her. No way was he ready for that.

Vectra's management crew called her over, demanding she join them in several of the photos. Laughter and good cheer abounded. Minka managed to lose herself in the moment and have a better time than she'd expected. When she left the group, it was to take a turn about the room with Austin, who had come over to rave about the turnout.

"Well, everyone had a hand in it, Austin. No way are you heaping all that credit on my head," Minka playfully scolded.

"That may be, but you put it all in place. Ask anyone." He turned his bright stare toward the noisy room. "They all say you were their go-to girl. The one who made sure the right people connected."

Minka was genuinely pleased by the comments, and silently, she noted that her time with Qasim would end on a high note. Austin began leading her to the crowded dance area.

A talented quartet began their next set with a pro-

vocative bluesy tune that eased into a mellower mood.
The seamless shift in tempo was a welcome respite from
the fast-paced excitement of the evening.

"I hope your clients are impressed by their potential
new digs," Minka said.

"No longer *potential*, Ms. Gerald. I was just upstairs
signing the last of the paperwork. The clients are totally
happy and totally vested. Everything has been sold."

"Austin!" Delighted, Minka tugged the sleeve of the
man's gray silk shirt and leaned in for a hug. She kissed
Austin's cheek, and he reciprocated with a peck to hers.
He dipped her and then swung her into an energetic
twirl that spun her right into the arms of another.

"Oliver," she said breathlessly. She glanced back to
scan for Austin, who blew her a kiss as he disappeared
into the heavy crowd.

"Sorry," Oliver said once their eyes met again.

"It's okay…" Her voice still carried traces of vampy
breathlessness. Minka was all too aware of the way her
breasts vivaciously heaved at the scooped neck of her
chic turquoise jumper.

"Sorry," she said, unaccustomed to feeling quite so
flustered.

Oliver's brilliant stare harbored a meaningful hunger. "An apology is definitely not necessary."

He leaned in and took her lips, his tongue taking
complete possession of hers.

The claiming, drugging, ravenous kiss wiped her
mind clear of everything aside from what existed between them in that moment. Whimpers marked her torment, a sensuous torment that ruptured into splinters
of desire.

Oliver's own whimpers erupted in a lower key, but

one that was just as sensuously tormented. Minka shivered and nuzzled in to absorb more of the kiss.

Faintly, through the haze of mounting arousal, Minka heard someone commend the way Oliver handled her. She moaned his name, making a weak attempt to encourage him to cool it.

Oliver, knowing her moan was meant to dissuade him, simply cupped her jaw to keep her where he wanted her. His moan was a brief, yet firm directive that she forget any plans she may've had for bringing an end to their kiss, or anything else between them.

His fingertips strummed a lazy tune along her jaw that kept time to the languid strokes of his tongue. "You still have to go tonight?" he asked between the slow, lusty thrusts.

"Yeah…" Her fingers tightened on the collar of his midnight-blue jacket.

Oliver released a ragged sigh. "Damn my sister for not thinking to put a hotel in this place."

Minka wanted to laugh, but thought twice when she noticed his stony, unreadable expression.

"When can I see you?" he asked.

"Anytime. Just give me a call."

The airy, no-expectations way she responded only seemed to sharpen Oliver's stoniness. Minka felt a withering sensation take root in the depths of her stomach and could think of nothing to say that might ease his mood.

"Oliver? Seriously, just call, okay?" she repeated when he continued to glare.

"You don't really expect me to, do you?"

Her expression gave her away.

Oliver inclined his head, as though considering a new

possibility. "Maybe you're hoping I won't call. Maybe it's both."

"Oliver…" She gripped his collar tighter. "I believe you."

"It's okay, Mink. I'd think I was full of it too." His striking stare wandered lovingly across her face. "You know I plan to give you every reason to take me for my word, but the rest will be on you. You'll have to decide whether you want to give me a real chance." He shrugged. "If my call isn't returned, I guess I'll have my answer. I won't like it, but I'll accept it. You can trust me on that."

She opened her mouth, not knowing what to say. It didn't matter.

"Need a ride to the airport?" Oliver asked. "Don't want you to miss your flight."

"Oh, no, the—" She almost told him that the plane wouldn't leave until she got there. Zena had arranged for one of the BGI private jets to bring her back to San Francisco.

"I already rented a car, and it's outside. My stuff's already in there."

"Nice." The corners of his delectable mouth turned downward. "You're really ready to get the hell out of here, aren't you?"

"I just need a day to unwind before getting back to work."

"Unwind." Oliver nodded. "Because you just can't do that in Miami, right?"

Obvious regret clouded Minka's dark face, but she knew it would be hopeless to explain.

Oliver didn't push for a reply—he knew he'd gotten his point across. Smiling softly, he dropped a kiss to the corner of her mouth and let his lips linger there. "Be safe," he said. He offered Minka his arm and escorted her back to the gallery's main floor, where he left her.

"Unwind…" Minka was recalling her use of the word and grimacing at what a laugh that was. She'd been nothing but *wound up* since returning to California. Her planned Sunday of leisure had been spent regretting and second-guessing everything she'd said to Oliver the night she left Miami.

She was afraid. So what? She could at least admit that in the privacy of her own mind. Oliver Bauer was enough to frighten any woman. Why had he singled her out to receive the windfall of his affections? She'd been happy living her life and enjoying the social circle she'd built for herself.

Minka snorted a laugh. "Right." She sighed to round out the gesture. Shaking her head, she put her focus where it needed to be and grabbed the chocolate leather tote from the passenger seat of her Benz. She paused to give herself a once-over through the car window and then sprinted up the wide driveway leading to her grandmother's home. She navigated the walkway with effortless grace, wearing spiked heels that emphasized the shapeliness of her legs beneath the pencil skirt that accentuated her bottom.

The phone buzzing inside the tote roused a hissed curse. Minka slowed her steps while digging out the mobile. She had no intentions of taking the call but wanted to silence the device so that it wouldn't be a disruption during the meeting. However, the number that showed up prompted an answer.

"Will. Not hiding behind untraceable phones this

time? What gives?" There was silence, and Minka thought he might not answer. "I can see your name and number on my phone."

"I know you can," Will replied at last. "I wanted you to know you didn't bring me to my knees when you got Sim to fire me."

"Your scheming got you fired, Will."

"It's water under the bridge." He sounded calm. "I'm back on top, and all is right in the world."

"Ah, I see, found a new company to extort money from, huh?"

"You're a nosy twit, Minka. Someone's gonna do something about that one day."

"Oh? Will that be you? I'm hoping so."

"Trust me, you wouldn't want that."

"I don't want what, Will?" Minka continued to goad the man, her agitation fueled by her own stress. "A lot of big talk from a liar who betrays his friends?"

"Easy, Minka." The calm in Will's voice harbored a decided edge. "You don't have Qasim to run interference for you anymore—he's got a new woman to take care of. And besides, I'm not part of his payroll now, remember?"

"Hmph, I never needed Qasim to have my back against the likes of you. In fact, I was a little pissed that he didn't let me fire you myself when you betrayed him. Screw with me, Will, and I promise I won't miss out on the chance again." She ended the call, clipping Will's rebuttal.

Minka silenced the phone and dropped it in the tote. She gave herself a minute to gather her wits and continued her trek toward the front door. She did a double-take, noticing a gleaming Jeep Wrangler near the top of the drive, but she didn't slow her walk until she'd reached the double oak doors trimmed in beveled glass.

"There you are!" Fiona McMullen met her boss's granddaughter in the foyer. "Your grandmother's about to have lunch with your guests—hurry, child."

Minka took no offense to the woman's scolding. It was difficult to talk sass to someone who had changed your diapers. "How long have they been here?" she asked.

"Almost half an hour."

Minka gave a nod and secured the tote strap in her grip. Fiona tugged it free.

"None of that," Fiona said. "There's no business talk till after lunch. Mr. Bauer is an old friend, and your Gram wants to catch up with him."

Minka frowned. "Bauer? Oscar…Bauer?"

"Yes, yes." Fiona waved Minka on as though she were an annoyance. "They're out on the lanai. It's a lovely day—nice and cool. Your grandmother's arranged for lunch to be served there. The four of you should be eating in about twenty minutes."

Minka couldn't make her feet move. "The—the four of us?"

Fiona shook her head over Minka's dawdling. "Mr. Bauer and his son will be joining you and your grandmother. Now go, go."

Fiona left Minka in the front hall. Just as well, since she was sure to lose her famous Irish temper while Minka stood there dumbfounded.

She made a tentative effort at last. Her progress was slow, but gained momentum the closer she drew to the sunroom that opened up into a spacious stone lanai. The space allowed for the gorgeous landscape of Zena

Gerald's property to be enjoyed no matter the weather. Minka heard the woman's voice the moment she stepped out onto the lanai.

"Ah! Here's my girl!"

Oliver hoped he was doing an adequate job of masking his emotions when Zena Gerald greeted her granddaughter. He and his father stood when Zena left her chair to pull Minka into a hug.

Minka's focus was on Oliver, who stood only a few feet away.

"Miami obviously agreed with you, love. You're glowing!" Zena raved.

"Thanks, Gram." Minka felt heat rush to her cheeks and forced her gaze from Oliver to the handsome older man at his right. "Mr. Bauer, it's good to see you again."

Oscar moved to envelope Minka in a quick embrace. "Very good to see you too, Minka. Your grandmother's right; you're glowing and as lovely as usual."

"Thank you." Minka smiled.

"Minka, honey, have you met Oscar's son, Oliver?"

Oliver didn't give Minka the chance to respond. "We've met, Miss Zena." He took Minka's hand and pulled her in to brush his mouth over her cheek. He heard her sharp intake of breath, and his smile became more defined.

"We could've come back from Miami together if I'd known we were invited to the same meeting."

"Small world." Minka's demeanor held an airy, yet phony vibrancy.

"How wonderful!" Zena clasped her hands. "What a nice coincidence being in Miami at the same time."

"Uh, yes, we, uh, we were both there working on the project I was sent on for Wilder," Minka explained.

"I see." Zena's dark eyes sparkled merrily and illuminated her lovely oval face. "Well, this will make for a cozy meal. I can't wait to hear about everything you two got into down there."

Oliver's expression was devilry at its best. "It was work and play at its finest, Miss Zena."

"Now, I've *definitely* got to hear about it." Zena beamed at Oliver then sobered and took note of her granddaughter's quiet. "Baby?" She used the back of her hand to feel Minka's cheek and forehead. "Are you all right? A touch of jet lag, maybe?"

Minka had to smile over the concern. "I'm okay." She took Zena's hand and kissed it.

Oliver seemed oblivious to the intensity with which he watched Minka. The smile curving his mouth would have been hidden had he realized how closely his father was studying him.

"Zena?" Oscar caught the woman's attention. "Didn't you say something about a garden? Think we have time to look it over before lunch? I don't think I'll want to move much afterward."

Zena was always in the mood to show off the results of her latest hobby. "I think we've got time." She gathered the material of her flowing lime and powder-blue lounge dress in one hand, waving toward Minka with the other. "Baby, get yourself a drink and freshen Oliver's. We'll be back soon."

Zena and Oscar left, and soon, only the sound of chirping birds and the rustle of leaves remained.

"Are we done pretending now?" Oliver asked.

Chapter 13

"Can't believe I didn't put this together before," Minka said with a skeptical smile as she freshened Oliver's club soda. "Do you know how many black billionaires there are in the world?"

"Probably way more than we know of."

Minka nodded.

"How is it no one knows?" Oliver shook his head as though not quite believing it himself. "How do you know my dad?"

"Your dad's been handling my grandparents' real-estate interests for years, but it was only a few months ago that I met him when I went to see Vectra at his place in SoMa."

"Did Vectra know?"

Minka shook her head. "Not then—your dad didn't even put it together when we met that day. Sim told Vectra right after we left for Miami."

Oliver took the drink Minka passed him and began to walk the lanai. Absently, he studied the table that had been set invitingly.

"So Qasim, he, um, he knows."

Oliver hadn't exactly phrased a question but Minka nodded anyway. "My granddad was one of his first clients, and he was the biggest. My grandfather kind of took Sim under his wing, let him cut his teeth on a few million dollars."

Oliver grinned. "Cut his teeth on a few million, huh?"

Minka had to smile at the phrasing as well. "They loved Sim like he was their own."

"And they trusted you with him," Oliver said.

"Yeah." Minka's expression was reflective. "They understood that I wanted to make my own way. Sim was building his company, so that gave me the chance to earn my stripes."

"Why didn't you tell me?"

Minka sipped from her club soda. "I didn't want you to change."

Oliver reclined against one of the stone columns. His expression was coaxing.

Minka took a spot against an opposing column. Resting her head back on it, her dark gaze took on a whimsical gleam as she scanned the lanai.

"I like the way men treat me when they don't know."

Oliver cleared his throat and forced his attention to the contents of his glass. "What way is that?" he asked, working doggedly to dismiss the stab of something powerfully possessive at her mention of the way *men* treated her.

Minka left the column and paced while considering her response. Oliver soothing himself by taking in the fluid way she moved. He fantasized about her locking her legs around his back while those heels still adorned her feet.

"They treat me like I'm just me—just…plain ol' Minka who works as a secretary at a brokerage firm."

"Ah…" Oliver swigged down some soda. "You mean, poor ol' Minka who tries to hide in corners and act like she's got no idea how she affects men?"

"I know well enough. Why do you think I stick to the plain-ol'-Minka role?"

"Because you don't really trust any of the men you see? How's that working for you?"

"I don't date men because I'm looking for a soul mate. Companionship is a lovely thing, Oliver."

"What? Someone to go to the movies with? That's all you want from a guy?"

"That's about all I expect. I've done the 'search for a soul mate' thing. But that journey tends to veer off in one of two ways once the 'soul mate' discovers I'm one of *the* Geralds."

"Tell me how it…veers off?" Oliver abandoned his stance against the column and moved closer to Minka.

"They either go overboard with the wooing because they've got visions of money dancing in their heads." She smiled over the imagery. "*Or*, they leave, because they hate the idea of becoming a kept man who has to beg his wife for money to go out with the boys."

"Come on, Mink…" He intentionally purred the phrase, loving that it clearly affected her. "You think that I would do that to you?"

"No, Oliver."

"Then why—"

"Oliver, you're different, okay? I've...I've never met anyone like you before."

"So none of your other suitors came from money?"

"That's not what I mean."

"Then what?"

"The things you said to me."

Oliver chuckled, drained his glass. "You mean those things that made you think I was completely out of my mind?"

Minka was already shaking her head. "That's why they affected me the way they did. You had no reason to say them. I'd already told you how much I wanted to sleep with you."

"Mmm-hmm, right before you said you didn't want a relationship with someone you had business ties to." He raised his glass to the ceiling. "I'm pretty sure this qualifies, babe."

"Oliver—"

"Why didn't you tell me before you left Miami?"

"Because I want to keep seeing you."

"What for?" He leaned in, allowing her to see his irritation. "I told you I wasn't in this for a fleeting companionship. I can get that anywhere." His startling stare made a few more sweeps of her body. He shook his head, looking as though he were still in shock. "I should've known there was something," he muttered.

"Something?"

Oliver set down his glass, made a move as if to loosen his tie but then seemed to recall he wasn't wearing one. "I couldn't figure out what it was about you that kept tugging at me. Something about the way your mind works, your demeanor." He laughed shortly, skirting the line between humor and frustration. "You're walking sexuality, and you don't seem to know it." He shook his head in wonder as he looked her over. "You have poise under pressure, and you never show too much of your hand." He shrugged. "Guess that's a testament to the way you were raised. Whatever it is, it's not like anything I've ever known. That's quite a declaration for a man like me, Minka."

"So I'm a novelty?" she asked.

"Don't do that." Temper flashed in his riveting stare. "Don't try to make it seem insignificant." He began to walk toward her. "I admit that having you come apart on me when I'm inside that body of yours is beyond erotic." He smiled, noticing her sharp inhalation in response to his words.

He closed more of the distance between them. "Minka, do you know that it's damn near impossible for me to keep my mind on anything else once I know you're in the same room with me?"

She smiled, moved away from the column before he could trap her there. "That's only infatuation..."

"You could be right, but I really don't know what to make of this since I've got nothing to compare it to."

"So I'm research?" she teased.

Oliver closed his eyes while muttering a curse. "Are you being difficult on purpose?" he asked.

Minka faltered a step. "No, Oliver. I'm just trying to keep myself from getting my hopes up."

"And you're counting on being disappointed."

"No. No, I don't want that at all."

"Yet you refuse to give me a real chance, even when I tell you how I feel about you."

"What's the challenge, Oliver?" Minka moved her

hands away from her body. "Trying to see how long it'll take to break me?"

His expression was a mix of playful danger and subtle arrogance. "I've already broken you. Maybe I'm waiting to see how long it'll take you to admit that." He paused. "I know my relationship track record is crap, Minka, but it's not everyday that I tell a woman I'm in love with her."

"Dammit, Oliver." She sighed. "I'm in love with you too. But as you just said, your relationship track record is crap, and mine is definitely a laugh fest. I'd love to share your optimism that this'll lead to happily-ever-after, but I guess I'm too busy trying to make sure my heart doesn't get shredded. Dammit." The pressure of tears built behind her eyes, and she turned her back.

Oliver approached and turned her to face him. "Does it help to know I'm scared too?"

"You?" she blurted in a voice heavy with emotion.

Oliver smiled at her disbelief. "It happens."

Minka sniffed, her eyes fixed on his muscular neck. "It's not the same," she said.

"Why? Because I've got a string of women at my beck and call to make it all better afterwards?"

She gave a weak laugh. "Don't you?"

"I know a lot of women, Minka, but as for them making things all better, that hasn't been true in a long time. Way before I knew you existed." He used his thumb to dry a tear clinging to the corner of her eye. "I get that this is different for you, that it'll affect you differently than it will me." He moved a little closer. "Just know it's not easy for me either, Mink. I wasn't looking for a real relationship when we met. But it's not just about curiosity for me. I'd very much like for you to believe that."

He kissed her, a mere peck, but Minka reeled from its intensity just the same. He was straightening and moving away when Oscar's and Zena's voices filled the air as they returned to the lanai. Lunch was served moments later.

"So since the two of you already have a rapport, Oliver, I thought it'd be just wonderful to let you start working on new strategies for the account," Zena said once her guests had their fill of the big lunch the kitchen staff had supplied. Conversation had covered everything from Zena's gardening to all the fun to be had in Miami.

Oliver was undoubtedly pleased by the idea of the new partnership. "If it's okay with Mink, it sounds good to me."

Zena nodded keenly. She'd noted that Oliver had shortened Minka's name and that Minka was oddly tense and emotional.

"Well, then, I'll leave it to the two of you to work out an arrangement."

Minka emerged from her daze in time to catch her grandmother's coy expression. Thankfully, Zena didn't seem in the mood to press for details. She'd already moved on to other business and was making sure Oscar and his people would be on hand for the upcoming stockholders' meeting. Zena extended a special invite to Oliver, and he graciously accepted.

"Splendid!" Zena clapped her delicate hands and beamed at Oliver. "The highlight of the evening will be my official announcement recognizing Minka as my new successor."

"Gram—"

"Hush." Zena raised a hand without looking in her granddaughter's direction. "Everyone already knows that I seek your input and advice on company business." She looked at Minka. "Everyone recognizes your skill except you, Sweet-thing. The stockholders know how highly I value your opinions as well as the successes you've brought to the company. All this on top of the fact that you've got a full plate with Wilder."

"It will most likely be easier to run a multi-billion dollar corporation than turn down your grandmother, Minka," Oliver said.

They all laughed, dispelling the tension that had been brewing.

"Well, Z, I've got a meeting to prepare for." Oscar extended a hand toward Zena. "Walk me out by way of your garden?"

"I'd love to!" Zena eagerly accepted Oscar's hand. "Minka, take care of Oliver until I get back."

"Miss Z., I've got to be going too," Oliver said.

"Oh, poo." Zena pouted for a moment before smiling Minka's way. "You don't mind showing Oliver out, do you, love?"

Minka stood while Zena rounded the table to envelope Oliver in a hug. She gave him final orders to be in attendance for the stockholders' meeting then set off with Oscar to the gardens.

"Your grandmother's somethin' else," Oliver said.

"You have no idea."

"Will you make me wait until the stockholders' meeting to see you again?"

"What for?" Minka shrugged. "My grandmother already knows something's up."

"Yeah." Oliver smirked. "I'm pretty sure my dad does too."

"Will this put a cramp in your style?" Minka fixed him with a leering stare.

Oliver gave a dismissive shrug. "Most women I know don't take me for a one-woman guy. They'll just assume you're—"

"Another of your harem?" She finished with a playful smile.

"Sorry."

"Don't be. Most of the people you're likely to meet will think you're with me for my money and assume *you're* just—"

"Another gigolo?"

"Sorry." Minka grinned. "We're quite a pair, huh?"

"We could be." No playfulness tinged Oliver's words. He stepped closer, cornering her near the lanai's entryway.

"Oliver—"

"No more hiding," he said seconds before his mouth touched hers.

The kiss was a provocative mix of sweetness and sensuality. His tongue pursued hers with deliberate teasing lunges that coaxed needy whimpers from her. When she whined his name, he chuckled softly.

"Come see me tomorrow? My office?"

"Are we going to have a meeting?" Disappointment colored her words.

Again, he laughed. "You could say that. Come see me?"

She nodded.

"Good girl."

He put a lingering open-mouthed kiss to her neck and walked away, leaving her reeling in dissatisfaction.

"Is that what you're looking for?" Lorna Spikes looked from the laptop to her friend's scowling face.

"This is good work, Lorna. I definitely have what I was looking for."

"Mind clueing me in?"

"He's there."

Lorna inclined her head, brown eyes narrowing. "That doesn't go a long way in clueing me in."

Minka was still scowling at the laptop's screen. "What are you doing over there, snake?"

"Minka! You're scaring me. What the hell is going on?"

"I think Will Lloyd's up to his old tricks again."

Lorna twirled a thin braid around her fingertip. "I'm drawing a blank on the name."

"He worked for Qasim until a few months ago. Sim had reason to believe the guy was stealing money from a charity fund. We then caught him red-handed, and he was fired."

"So...explain to me why this fool is working for one of our subsidiaries and not sporting the latest in orange jumpsuits?" Lorna asked after several silent moments.

Minka sighed, pushing away from the desk at her home office. "Against my better judgment, Sim decided not to press charges. He just wanted the man out of Wilder."

"That doesn't sound like Qasim."

"Well...the guy's an old army buddy. Saved Sim's life once."

"Admirable." Lorna nodded from her relaxed spot

on the sofa. "And understandable that Sim wouldn't want to see the guy behind bars...but you still believe he shouldn't be trusted?"

"I *know* he shouldn't be trusted."

"Based on the embezzlement?"

"Based on the fact that he's been making calls to me—somewhere he just sits on the line and says nothing, others where we've had a few...choice words... for one another. He blames me for bringing an end to his scam."

"Have you lost your damn mind?" Lorna's voice was almost inaudible with disbelief. "Have you gone to the police?"

"I've got Walter Penner on it. He's the one who traced the calls back to a hotel in Salinas."

"Ah..." Realization was dawning for Lorna. "And the police?"

Minka stood and walked a short path behind her desk. "I don't want the sleaze in jail for making prank calls, Lorna. I want him in jail for embezzlement."

"But Sim isn't pressing charges."

"Sim won't, but I would."

Lorna whistled. "Min...what you're talking about... it's entrapment."

"It would be, but I won't have to lift a finger to set any traps for Will. Chances are he's already working overtime on a way to screw with Calvin Spring's company. All I've got to do is wait."

"You sound pretty confident this guy'll do something that stupid."

Minka sat on the edge of the maple desk. "It's who he is—he thinks he's smarter than everyone else."

"And is it wise to taunt someone like that? An *ex-military* someone?"

"As aggravated as I was over Sim's decision to let Will get off, I accepted it. But now he's working for Calvin Spring. It's an investment firm, remember?" She watched Lorna nod. "It's not as powerful as Wilder, but it could entice someone like Lloyd to dip into money that's not his."

Lorna leaned forward on the sofa. "I take it you haven't shared any of this with Miss Z. yet either?"

"No...but I only just confirmed Will's employment with a BGI subsidiary, so—"

"Minka, stop." Lorna left the sofa. "Save that weak explanation for Miss Z. It'll be fun to watch her rip you apart over it."

"I don't need her upset over this, Lorna."

"Which you know she would be, and for good reason. Why do you have to take this guy down yourself?"

"Dammit, Lorna, I'm about to be the head of a multi-billion-dollar organization. If I can't take down a thief, what does that say about my business prowess?"

Lorna waved off the reasoning. "Not buying it," she sang.

Minka held her head in her hands. "Lorn...if I had just waited before going to Qasim with this, that idiot would've probably put his foot in it so deep that Sim would've had no choice but to put him in jail."

"Minka?" Lorna took a step toward her friend and then hesitated. "You aren't blaming yourself for a decision that Qasim made, are you?"

"No, but I don't think I can sit by and see him get away with it again. Especially since he's now targeting me for revenge."

Lorna seemed more horrified the longer her friend spoke. "You really believe money is all he's after, Min? This sounds personal. What if he wants to get closer than calling you on the phone?"

"Just set up the meeting with Calvin Spring, all right?" Minka pleaded. "I'll get Will Lloyd out of my life before any of that happens."

"On your own?"

"Yes, Lorn!" Minka closed her eyes, seeking to calm her heavy agitation. "I have to prove I can handle difficult situations."

"And you think going off on your own Billie Badass mission is gonna prove that?" Lorna shook her head forebodingly. "Your grandfather didn't get where he did by playing the lone wolf. It's okay to ask for help, Min. A shoulder to lean on can be a lovely thing."

"I'll keep that in mind." Minka gave a resolved sigh. "Now can we discuss how I want to handle this conversation with Calvin Spring? I could *really* use your *help* in tweaking it."

Lorna caught the sarcasm and groaned. "If you insist."

Chapter 14

"It sounds like fun, Vectra. I've been dying to get out there and see the vineyard at night."

Vectra's laughter came through the other end of the phone line. "Trust me, it's an incredible sight. So we'll have dinner on the terrace facing the west vineyard. The sky is incredible even long after the sun sets. It'll be a great view for dining."

"Well, count me in." Minka laughed.

"Yes!" Vectra sounded as if she were clenching a triumphant fist on the other end of the line. "Okay, so we'll get started around eight. Does that give you enough time to get out here?"

"Should be fine. I've only got one meeting, since my boss has been in a strangely good mood lately. He gave me a few extra days off after Miami."

"Wow...wonder what *that's* about?"

Minka smiled over the blatant sarcasm in Vectra's voice. "I'm sure I have you to thank, but I'm not about to question it. See you around eight."

The call ended and Minka expelled a deep breath. She was at Oliver's office for the first time. His work space paid distinct homage to his love of architecture. The rich wood paneling accentuated the black wood framework of photographs, and an inviting array of sofas and armchairs hugged corners, making for cozy nooks in the busy work space. Lamps hugged those spaces as well as the main desk and additional drafting tables the room boasted. Minka's impromptu tour led her into a kitchen/living area along the office's second level. She wanted to sink into the bliss promised by the oversized suede sofas of rich earth tones that complemented the carpeting beneath.

"How do you like it?"

She turned sharply at the sound of Oliver's voice. "Sorry for snooping—your admin wasn't specific about what parts of your office were off-limits."

Oliver grinned. "That's because nothing's off-limits to you. How do you like it?"

"It's fantastic." Minka turned to observe the space again. "You can work, play, sleep, eat, everything from here."

"Yeah." Oliver looked pleased. "That was the plan when I designed the place."

"Uh-oh." Minka looked wounded. "Please tell me that you don't spend your nights here on the regular?"

"Afraid I do."

"Hmm…that doesn't sound like the playboy I've heard of."

"I'm highly misunderstood, Ms. Gerald."

"Well." Minka's voice and expression held a refreshing air. "You've got me here now. Where do you want to get this strategy session started?"

Oliver was the one to appear wounded that time. "Is that the impression I gave when I asked you over?"

Minka smiled curiously. "It was pretty much all my grandmother talked about during lunch."

"Oh, I think she had her reasons. And not all of them were business related."

Minka laughed. "You caught that too, huh?" She folded her arms across the lavender wrap blouse she wore. "And you know that your dad wasn't fooled either."

"I wasn't trying to fool him."

"We should focus on what we're here for."

"Good idea." Oliver seemed strangely pleased. He promptly crossed the room to relieve Minka of the work tote she carried.

"I'm going to your sister's for dinner."

"Why?" The news gave Oliver pause.

She smiled. "To eat? That's usually what happens when you're invited to dinner."

Muttering a curse, Oliver rubbed his fingers through the curls at his nape. "Prepare yourself for a lecture on what a bad relationship choice you're making."

"That's crazy. Your sister loves you." Minka made herself comfortable on an amber lounge chair.

"I know." Oliver smiled as Vectra's image came to mind. "But the idea of me in a relationship gives her plenty cause for concern."

"Why do you think that is?"

Oliver eased a hand into his trouser pocket and shrugged. "She's got her reasons."

"Valid reasons?"

"Oh, yeah."

"But you still don't agree with them?"

"I tend not to agree with things that hinder me from getting what I want."

"*Want* is future tense, isn't it? You've already had me."

"I want to keep you, Mink."

"Hmm…" She cast a lingering stare toward the ceiling. "I'm not sure I can be kept."

Oliver didn't return her teasing smile. "I'm serious."

A series of dings pinched the air from Oliver's cell phone. He cursed the interruption but gave a resigned smile when he checked the display. "Vec? Just talkin' about you." Curiosity took hold of his features suddenly, and a few seconds passed.

"What's the occasion for inviting me to this dinner, and will I be PO'd at the end of it?"

"You'll just have to come and see."

"What's up your sleeve, Vecs?"

"You'll have to come and see. Will you?"

Oliver studied Minka for a few seconds and then grimaced and nodded. "I'll be there. What time?" He nodded again and then hung up.

"Guess who's coming to dinner?"

Her smile was sweet. "I told you there was nothing to worry about."

"I don't know how you figured that," he said with a scowl.

"Well, if it helps, we can pretend there's nothing going on."

Oliver's scowl deepened. "Why in the hell would you think that'd make me feel better?"

"I just meant..." Minka cut short her explanation when she realized it was doing more harm than good.

Oliver's scowl remained in place, its darkness appearing to intensify when he joined Minka on the lounge chair. "I didn't ask you here to talk business." His voice held a calm that belied the fierceness of his expression. "I have no plans to act like I don't know you." His stirring gaze took a quick, heated trip down the length of her.

"Okay." Her heart was in her throat as her expectations mounted. She began to speak and then seemed to think better of it.

"What?" Oliver dipped his head to urge her to continue.

Minka focused on her hands in her lap. "I have to leave here soon to head right out to Vectra's if I plan to make it on time."

"Don't worry, I won't take long with you."

Expectation had Minka's heart dancing from her throat to her stomach. "I just don't, don't think I'll have time for a shower."

Oliver erupted into laughter then. If he hadn't known it before, he knew it then. The woman had completely endeared herself to him.

"Is that funny?" she asked in a small voice.

"I can't get over how precise you are."

She conceded with a shrug. "It's the mark of a good admin."

Curiosity took hold of his gorgeous features. "Why *that* job? It's a noble one for sure, but you could've come on board as a VP or something. Sim would've probably created a position for you."

Minka looked ready to laugh. "Not all billionaires

have massive egos, you know? I guess it's all about that plain ol' Minka persona I wanted to build. Besides, as Sim's admin I'm not restricted by the expectations of a title. Being an admin is more freeing."

"Your family did an excellent job raising you." He rubbed one of her curls between his thumb and index. "I've known women with far less who expect far more."

She smiled.

Oliver dropped a hand to his knee as if he'd suddenly recalled something. "You haven't seen every room in this place, have you?"

"I..." Minka looked bewildered. She accepted Oliver's hand when he offered it.

Together, they walked in silence, taking a short spiral staircase at the rear of the living area.

"Oliver, where...? Oh. Oh...wow."

Oliver stopped at the door frame and let Minka walk ahead. He enjoyed the sight of her strolling the bath. By then, he was sure she thought he and his sister had some weird obsession with bathrooms. He smiled, watching as she ran her fingers across the sink's brass fixtures and the glossy dark oak finish of the privacy panel shielding the toilet area at the far end of the room.

The cabinets were inlaid with mirrors and had Minka imagining what it'd be like to make love in such a place. The idea hit her out of nowhere, and she shook her head to try ridding herself of it. Oliver was still leaning against the door frame, but she felt as if he were much closer.

She rested against the oak counter space and studied the skylight above without really seeing it. Her mind was clearly on other things. It was a heady feeling to know that the man every woman wanted, wanted her.

Oliver pushed off the jamb and joined her at the counter. Gently, he tugged Minka to her feet and directed her to stand before him while he took her spot on the counter.

"This is convenient," she marveled at the room, her dark eyes alight with amusement. "Comes in handy when you entertain, I guess?"

Oliver took no offense, merely making a tsking sound as he made slow work of appraising her body beneath his gaze. "There you go thinking the worst of me again. This is where I work, Minka. I never *entertain* here."

She swallowed, faintly arching into the slow outline his thumb was making around the curve of her breast. "What's this, then?"

He smiled. "This is me changing that fact."

"You've put a lot of thought into this place," she said as he began undressing her.

"I did," Oliver said softly. "It takes proper attention to bring any space alive."

Minka sucked in a sharp breath. She dragged her eyes from the high, open ceiling to Oliver, who had used an expert's touch to relieve her of the lavender blouse and bra. Her fingers lightly cradled the back of his head, her nails tangling just barely in the soft, chestnut forest of his hair. His head dipped and moved as he licked and suckled her nipples, using a tireless rhythm that forced needy moans from her throat.

Oliver cupped one of the dark mounds, and he used his free hand to lower the back zipper of the creamy beige skirt that hugged her hips and ample bottom. Lacy lavender panties followed soon after.

The garments pooled at Minka's pumps, just as Oliver stood and lifted her free of the crumpled fabric. He put her in the spot he'd just vacated on the counter. Minka didn't react to her bare bottom against the surface. Her skin was too sensually heated to be jarred by any chill.

Oliver remained clothed, and kept her still for an exploring kiss.

Minka moaned his name amidst the hungry assault his tongue subjected hers to. Oliver didn't seem to hear her as the kiss intensified.

He returned to fondle one nipple while his other hand insinuated itself between her thighs, open and quivering on either side of his body. His middle finger commenced a sweet stroking of her sex—once, twice, three times—before delving between the silken folds to the abundant moisture pooled at her center.

Minka's response was caught between a moan and a gasp. Her tongue lost the ability to even thrust back against his, she was so enraptured. Clutching his heavily muscled forearms, she began to work herself against his sex, potently rigid behind his zipper. She craved release in the deep, intimate caress. His stance between her legs, however, prevented much movement.

"Oliver—"

"Shh...I'll get you nice and cleaned up when I'm done." He stimulated her center beneath his thumb and grinned when she whimpered. "Trust me?" he asked.

Minka nodded obediently, finding contentment in clenching her walls about his deliciously intrusive finger. She arched up for another kiss, and he didn't disappoint her. They were in the depths of one that was more forceful, more possessive, when he suddenly withdrew.

"Oliver, no," she almost sobbed, lashes fluttering to stare at him accusingly.

"Shh…" He dipped his head, helping himself to another decadent, deliberate suckle at her nipples.

Minka faintly locked in on the sound of crinkling foil and opened her eyes to observe that his trousers were down and his boxers were midway around his powerful thighs. He used his teeth to tear into the foil wrapping of a condom. He made quick work of applying protection and then he was claiming her body with his. Minka was as overwhelmed by the sheer delight of that sensation as she was by her current position perched atop the counter without a stitch of clothing while Oliver managed to maintain more of his own.

Minka yearned to see him bared to her gaze and set out to unbutton his shirt. The task was difficult, considering her hands shook madly with increasing instability.

Oliver held Minka's thigh near his waist. He squeezed her hip in a viselike grip that would've warranted complaint had Minka not been so strongly aroused by the mastery of it.

Oliver rested his forehead to Minka's shoulder and inhaled her fresh, airy fragrance as though the aroma held a life-giving element.

The room's high ceiling caused their gasps, groans and cries to echo. They were encapsulated in an oasis of passion where they would have been content to remain.

"So you think we're a good match?"

Will nodded while setting his briefcase on the passenger seat of the rental he'd driven into San Francisco. He had just met with Armor Medical, the company being considered to take over the health care for Spring Holdings employees.

"I've got a good feeling about them." Will spoke into his mobile.

"Sounds good."

"Trust me, sir, their documentation was very thorough. I've got the tired eyes to prove it."

Spring chuckled heartily from his end of the line. "Get yourself a good meal and check in somewhere for a good night's sleep, man. You've earned it."

"Thank you, sir, but I thought I'd drive back to Salinas so I can be at the office early tomorrow to present a formal report on Armor."

Spring laughed with renewed vigor. "Now I know I've made the right decision in hiring you! Consider tomorrow a day off."

"Thanks, sir, but no."

"I insist. Hell, I'm planning on a day off myself. I've got one last phone conference, and I'm calling it quits."

"Could I be of help with any of that, sir?"

"Nah, it's just routine stuff with the HR Director and new head of BGI—we became a subsidiary of theirs after the merger. The president's granddaughter will be assuming control of the business by the end of the year. You should come with me to meet the rest of the executive team at the upcoming stockholder meeting."

"Sounds like a big event," Will said.

"It definitely is, and it's as good a time as any to show you off. I'm grooming you for great things, man."

"Thank you, sir."

"Thank me by getting some rest and enjoying that day off," Spring said. "We'll talk soon."

Carro Vineyards, Saint Helena, CA

Minka put her car in park and smiled at the thought of her afternoon with Oliver.

She had rushed from Oliver's office right to Wilder, where she and Lorna had agreed to meet for the conference call with CG Spring of Spring Holdings. Despite the seriousness of the call, Minka hadn't been able to get Oliver out of her mind. What woman could?

Oliver Bauer was a master at making a woman feel pampered, and he did it in a way that made her feel as if she was the only one. Minka knew she was beginning to believe that the man was serious about his feelings for her.

And her feelings for him?

She was in love with him—that was certain. But in love in the span of a couple weeks? That was fast even by adolescent standards, wasn't it?

He had loved her, showered with her, loved her again, and then ordered her to shower alone lest he'd never let her leave to get on with her day. Minka was thankful that the meeting with Spring had been by phone. The company president would've surely believed her to be rather strange.

The meeting had been productive, however. CG Spring had known nothing of the story behind Will Lloyd's departure from Wilder. Minka smiled lazily—at least now Spring knew that Will had worked for Wilder. She figured that was the golden nugget that had gotten Will hired at Spring Holdings. Lorna had done some digging on the Holdings president and discovered that anyone who knew Calvin Spring knew he had aspirations of his company being as big and busy as Wilder one day.

Minka heard a ding from her tote and recognized it as the reminder chime from her phone. She was already running about five minutes late to Vectra's dinner. The sun had already started to set, and there was a dusky effervescence to the air. Carro was indeed a charmed place, Minka thought. She decided to go for a stroll toward the main house. As she set off down the path, the shoulder strap of her tote snagged on what she assumed was a branch. Beautifully trimmed hedges were abundant and lined the wide walkway leading to the gold lit house in the distance. Minka halted to investigate the impediment. But when she turned, she found that it wasn't a branch to blame for the hindrance—it was William Lloyd.

Instinctively, Minka jumped back. As though he'd anticipated her move, Will caught her arm. The contents of her tote spilled to the ground as he gave her a harsh jerk back against him.

"Now, Minka, is that any way to treat a coworker?"

"We don't work together anymore, thief."

His smile was a snarl. "No we don't, do we? Thanks to you."

"Will—"

"Oh, it's all right, we're good. I'm very good. I'm finally someplace where I'm appreciated."

Will began tugging her along by the arm, as she squirmed to get free.

"I stopped by Wilder to tell you today, but I got there just in time to find you on your way out. I was hoping you were on your way home for the day." He gave her another brutal jerk. "So imagine my surprise when I discovered you were heading out to grand Carro. Getting chummy with Sim's rich dime piece, are we?"

Will wrenched Minka to a halt when they neared her car. He observed the Benz with a raised brow.

"I always wondered how you afforded this damn car. Was it a payoff from Sim for all your hard work of ridding Wilder of the riffraff?"

"You're an idiot." Minka winced, hearing her quick tongue before she could restrain it. "I bought my own car, and I don't need to boast about what I have or ride the coattails of others to get it."

Will looked livid and gave her another rough jerk that made Minka flinch at the abuse to her upper arm. Otherwise, she maintained her calm.

Will's smug demeanor returned. "You'll be pleased to know that I'm tugging myself right up the corporate ladder with a boss that recognizes a quality worker. He's a boss who doesn't look over my shoulder or take his cues from a secretary."

Relief began to course through Minka. She realized that Will didn't know yet about her talk with CG Spring. Spring had been outraged by his new employee's full background. Spring's parting words to Minka and Lorna had left no doubt that Will would soon be unemployed.

"Qasim didn't need my input," Minka spat. "He already had a thick file on your crimes, and he was just waiting for you to take it to a level that would ensure your incarceration for years." She noted the wild flare of Will's nostrils but wouldn't allow herself to be intimidated.

Will moved closer, moving a hand from one of Minka's

arms to cup it loosely around her neck. "So sweet of you to save me from prison…" He kissed her jaw.

Minka's skin crawled when his mouth moved from her jaw to her cheek. "I assure you I won't make that mistake again," she said.

Her words shifted Will back to his outraged state. He punished her with a vicious shaking, followed by another rough jerk that shielded Minka's gaze as thick locks of her hair fell forward into her face.

"You will do *nothing* again. Am I clear?" he snarled. "I don't look kindly on men who abuse women, but I'm beginning to see that sometimes it's a productive means to an end." With those words, he shook her again. "Am I clear?"

Minka didn't speak. Will moved closer, and she gasped, feeling his erection where he pressed in against her hip.

"Am I understood?" He breathed the question near her ear.

Minka nodded earnestly. "Yes."

"That's a good secretary," he cooed, kissing her ear before he shoved her to the ground.

Minka shrieked when her knees made contact with the gravel drive. She remained there, rendered immobile by fear and shock. She heard the sound of Will's retreating steps, the slam of a car door and the roar of an engine.

Will gunned the engine, and Minka screamed when he put the vehicle in drive and sped toward her. When the car was only a few feet away, Will made a sharp turn that sent flecks of dirt and rock flying in to her face. The car fishtailed, making its way off the property.

Chapter 15

Her heart surged and her breathing was labored, but she treasured the air that somehow managed to work its way through her lungs and out of her nostrils. Her thoughts were a blur, but somehow her brain moved her to get to safety.

She managed to push to her feet, wincing as pain splintered from her scraped palms up through her arms. On her feet at last, she stumbled toward the house. Her steps gained momentum, and soon she was slumping against the front door. She didn't bother with knocking, but twisted the knob and entered.

Minka left the door open and trudged into the foyer. How was her mind working? The sound of laughter faintly touched her ears. She moved in the direction it seemed to be coming from. She had lost one heel in the tussle, and now her other shoe sent an eerie, uneven

sound throughout the corridor that took her deeper into
the house.

The doorway at the end of the long hall led the way
into a huge sitting room. Minka discovered the laughter
was coming from her hostess. Vectra sat cuddled close
to Qasim, who was softly speaking with her.

Minka collapsed the instant Qasim and Vectra noticed her.

Oliver prayed for a quick end to that evening's dinner. He was in no mood to sit through a lecture from his
little sister. He knew her heart was in the right place,
but lectures weren't necessary. Not this time.

Minka Gerald had him wrapped around all ten of her
fingers. He knew it, knew without a hint of doubt, that
he was completely ruined for another woman. Despite
his very real reluctance, he'd been powerless to stop it.
He hadn't wanted to stop it.

He was driving in to Carro, smiling as he breathed
in the familiar and fragrant air that hinted of the area's
lustrous crop. The fragrance sustained him and never
failed to inspire his contentment.

He hadn't planned to arrive quite so late. When
Minka had left his office earlier that day, he'd men-
tally kicked himself for not finding a way to convince
her to stay. Instead, he'd thrown himself into his work,
deciding to finish up the most pressing matters of the
day. His plan? To take off with Minka the moment they
were done with Vectra's dinner.

They would spend the night at the place he kept there
at Carro. He'd take Minka to her place the following
morning to give her time to pack, and then it was off to
places unknown. He hoped her schedule would permit a

spontaneous trip, but he knew he'd take whatever time she'd give him. God, was he *that* far gone over her? The answer was an emphatic "yes." She had him, and Oliver found himself praying that she would want to keep him.

His contentment waned when he took the turn that would lead him to the main house. The flashing lights in the distance immediately set him on alert.

Oliver floored the gas and sent his Jeep speeding down the dirt road, pulling to a stop at the end of the driveway. Emergency vehicles bearing the Carro Vineyards logo clogged the driveway and much of the road beyond it.

He left the Jeep parked at a haphazard angle and ran for the house. Carro staff were in the yard, but Oliver paid them no mind as he barreled through. The front door was open, and he stormed inside, calling his sister's name as he moved down the hall.

Vectra emerged in the sitting room doorway.

"Vectra?" His pace quickened, and he didn't stop until he was jerking her off her feet and into his arms.

"I'm okay, I'm okay, Olive. Shh…" Vectra clenched her hands in his hair and kissed his cheek several times in reassurance. "I'm okay, honey."

Oliver heard the words but didn't truly believe them until he'd set Vectra to her feet and held her at a distance to observe her with his own eyes. "You're okay? What happened?" He glanced toward the others filling the area. "Why are they here? What…?"

"Honey, it's Minka."

Oliver's hands fell away from Vectra's arms as though they hadn't the strength to hold her any longer.

"Min…?" It was all he could manage before he staggered back as strength left his legs.

"Olive!" Vectra tried to support his weight yet failed miserably. Luckily, a few male guards came to her aid to take hold of Oliver.

"Where? Where is she?" His voice was a scratchy whisper.

Vectra smoothed a hand across his chest. "She's fine, honey. Let me take you to her."

The guards released Oliver, and he followed Vectra into the sitting room. Minka sat there next to Qasim on a sofa, looking small and defeated. Qasim held her arm, and her head rested on his shoulder. An EMS worker from the vineyard tended to one of the several nasty scrapes on her knee.

"Min?" Oliver's voice was still scratchy, but it carried in the busy room.

Minka blinked and lifted her head from Sim's shoulder as she searched the room.

"Oliver?" Her dark eyes filled, and soon tears were streaming down her cheeks.

Qasim left Minka's side to make room for Oliver. He squeezed the man's shoulder while Oliver claimed the spot. Minka turned her face into Oliver's chest and let emotion finally have its way.

She felt as though she'd been outside herself, barely able to recall her walk from the yard into the house. She heard someone say "shock" and guessed that was an apt description of her condition.

"It's all right, sweetie. It's all right, I'm here. I've got you…"

The words rumbled in Oliver's chest and brought her a sense of security she'd not felt since before her ordeal. Minka burrowed in closer to his chest and let the rest of the world drift away.

Silence held for a while until Oliver spoke, directing his words to his sister. "What the hell happened?"

"We don't know." Vectra rubbed her hands over her arms and looked totally bewildered. "She hasn't said a word. She walked in the house and just collapsed. They've been treating her wounds, but we've got no idea who's responsible for this."

"Security called right after she walked in here and passed out," Qasim said from his leaning stance against a tall armchair. "They reported a gray sedan speeding past the security gate, and they wanted to know if Vectra was all right."

Oliver nodded while taking in the recap. His striking features hardened into a mask as he absorbed the details. He looked down, squeezing the woman at his side. "Mink?" He kissed her temple and forehead. "Can you talk to me, babe?" He felt her stiffen in his arms. "Shh...it's over, you hear me? It's over, and I've got you. Can you tell me what happened?"

Minka pulled her face a few inches away from Oliver's chest. "It was Will."

The soft confession roused curses of rage from both Oliver and Qasim.

"It was Will Lloyd," Minka repeated. She rested her face against Oliver's chest again.

Vectra came to kneel beside the arm of the sofa. "Honey, what did he do?" she asked.

It took Minka some time to get out the explanation, but she told them everything, including the prank calls.

Carro's security chief was brought into the room to record Minka's statement.

"Ms. Gerald, did you see a license plate?"

"Why the hell don't you have it already?" Oliver snapped. "It's security protocol to record names, driver's licenses and tag numbers of everyone in or out of the gates at every entrance, right?" None of the staff piped up with a response. "Why wasn't that done?" he asked in a deceptively polite voice.

Again, there was no response.

"Did you at least record Ms. Gerald's information when *she* arrived? Who was on duty when this all went down?" Oliver continued.

The staff on hand visibly tensed.

"I believe there was a shift change," one of the deputies offered.

"Shift change between who?" The chief was already pulling up the information on his phone while he asked the question.

"Remember who's at fault here, Oliver," Vectra urged her brother while the guards were summoned.

Oliver slanted his sister a chilly stare. "Quiet," he ordered.

The guards arrived and the chief relayed the protocol questions that Oliver had previously raised. A round of finger-pointing ensued, which only heightened Oliver's and Qasim's agitation.

Qasim caught Vectra's eye. "Is this the top-notch security you kept bragging about?"

Chief of Security Spencer Hogan stepped forward. "With all due respect, Mr. Wilder..."

Vectra quickly surmised the heightening of emotion in the room. She saw Oliver's fist clench and Qasim's gorgeous dark features turn poisonous as the chief defended his men. "Spencer. Can we track the car based on what we *do* know?" Vectra asked, jumping up to ease the mounting tension.

Minka had gradually regained control of her faculties and was leaning forward to take part in the conversation. "He told me he'd been in San Francisco on business for his new job. He came to Wilder to gloat, saw me leaving and followed me here. His boss in Salinas confirmed that he'd sent him here for a meeting when I spoke to him by phone earlier today." Minka could feel Qasim's eyes boring into her as she shared the story. She forced herself to continue addressing the security chief. "Maybe he's driving a rental. If you contact CG Spring of Spring Holdings, he should know more on how to reach him."

The chief held a pen in his hand. "Would you happen to have a number for him, ma'am?"

"Oh." Minka's dismay renewed as she recalled the fate of her tote. "My bag is splattered out there on the drive. I—I'm not sure if my phone survived." From behind, she heard Oliver utter another furious curse.

"Thank you, Ms. Gerald. We'll contact the county PD and enlist their help to track down this coward."

"We appreciate whatever you can do." Vectra escorted the security team from the room. She returned moments later.

"Thanks for whatever you can do?" Oliver parroted his sister's words. "Why didn't you just tell 'em to take the rest of the week off?"

"Sure, Olive, that'll best help them find that jerk."

"I want 'em out, Vec—figure up their severance pay and get 'em the hell out of here."

"You want to fire our security team?"

"What part of 'I want 'em out' was unclear?"

"Oliver, you're just lashing out at them because you can't get your hands on Will."

"Oh, you caught that, did you?"

"Olive—"

"No, Vectra. If I'd fired their lax asses before this, maybe Lloyd would've at least been caught *before* he got off the property." Oliver's eyes blazed toward his sister. "Hell, they didn't even know the scum was here til he flew by them on his way out! He could've done anything to her out there.

"I can't believe that creep did this to you," Oliver fumed.

"Oliver, I'm okay, really," Minka said softly.

"Right," he breathed, "just like you were *okay* in Miami, hmm?"

Qasim, who had been quietly pacing the far side of the room, stopped. "What about Miami?"

Oliver's face beamed with fake surprise. "Well, hell, Sim, I see I'm not the only one kept out of the loop. Your boy came to Vectra's place when we were out there."

Once again, Qasim seared Minka beneath his dark, flat glare.

"What did he want?" Vectra asked her brother.

"Search me, but whatever it was, it wasn't anything I needed to worry over, was it, Mink?"

"Oliver—"

"Just like all the rest of his calls, right?" Oliver steamrollered Minka's explanation. "If that clown hadn't attacked you tonight, would you have ever said a damn word to me about him, Minka?"

Minka sat on the arm of the chair she stood closest to. "I thought I could handle it."

Oliver nodded as though her answer didn't surprise him. He shifted a quick, measuring look toward Vectra before looking back to Minka. "Of course you did. If I had a dime for every time I heard that—"

"Oliver!"

Oliver waved a hand in response to his sister's reproachful cry. He pushed off the sofa. "Don't think I'm in the mood for dinner. It'd be better if I just get the hell out of here."

"Oliver?" Minka stood, her voice hollow as unease barreled in at the thought of him leaving.

Oliver didn't acknowledge her call and walked out of the room.

"Oliver." Vectra prepared to go after her brother, but found her way blocked by Qasim.

"Stay with her." He looked to Minka. "I'll talk to him."

Vectra curled her fingers into the neckline of the midnight-blue tee he wore and rested her forehead to his jaw. "I'm sorry."

"Shh…" Qasim cupped her chin, waited for her eyes to meet his. "Enough of that." He kissed her forehead.

"Don't let him leave," Vectra urged.

"He's not goin' anywhere." Qasim looked to Minka who was on the chair and leaning forward, elbows braced to her thighs while she massaged her temples.

Qasim left to go after Oliver, and Vectra went to sit near the chair Minka occupied.

"What a day…" Minka groaned.

Vectra smiled. "If it helps, I can relate."

Minka replied with a sad smile. "I didn't mean to hurt Oliver."

"Honey." Vectra squeezed her hand. "You didn't do that."

"He didn't even want to come here tonight."

"Oh?"

"We've been…seeing each other since Miami."

Vectra nodded. "I kind of figured."

"He thought we'd be in for a lecture tonight. I told him he was wrong."

"No…he was right. Tonight was about more than that, but a lecture would've probably found its way in somewhere between dinner and dessert. The man knows me very well. But, um." Vectra massaged her eyes and then looked to Minka with a refreshed look. "I can see now that wouldn't have been necessary."

"Really?"

"I think I knew there was something different about him before you guys left for Miami. Did he tell you he already got the lecture from me?"

"No." Minka laughed. She recrossed her legs beneath her dirt-streaked cream skirt and leaned forward, eager to hear more.

Vectra relaxed into the sofa, her expression a bit whimsical. "I don't know…there's something about him. Something less…confident, and the man's got the utmost confidence when it comes to women."

"Easy to believe." Minka grinned.

"But I don't see all that when he talks about you or is around you. There's this little-boy uncertainty in place of that…arrogance. Like there's something he wants to know, but he's afraid to find out all the same."

"He says he's in love with me." Minka watched Vectra smile.

"Do you get how huge that is for him? Love isn't a word he uses lightly, not even with me and my dad. For him to share that with you…" Vectra shook her head in wonder. "He's jumped some pretty high hurdles to overcome those fears of his."

"I'm scared too, Vectra." Minka settled back into the chair. "He's seen more of who I am than I've ever let any man see. I don't know how this works."

Vectra fidgeted with a tassel on the crimson cap-sleeved blouse she wore. "If it makes you feel better, neither does he."

"My life is about to get all kinds of crazy, Vectra." Minka moved next to her on the sofa. "This situation with Will won't help."

"Don't shut him out, hon. Don't shut him out of any of it. Trust me on that."

Minka observed Vectra closely for a moment. "Is it my imagination, or was that discussion earlier about more than what happened with Will?"

Vectra looked down at her hands limply clenched in her lap. "I was in a relationship a long time ago… It turned abusive."

"Vectra…" Minka leaned over to squeeze Vectra's knee.

"It was pretty hard for my dad and Olive to see me go through that."

"I'm so sorry." Minka gave an encouraging smile.

Vectra nodded. "Thank you… Tonight was about Oliver remembering the days when I would tell him and my dad that I could handle it on my own and that I didn't need their help." She took a deep breath. "I don't think they'll ever truly forgive me for shutting them out the way I did. They didn't want me to feel…overpowered by a man, but I made them back off."

"Did it get uglier after that?" Minka asked.

"It got crazy enough, and what happened here tonight with you and Will was enough to spook Oliver and carry him right back to that time."

Minka looked to the door. "Do you think they'll find Will?"

Vectra looked to the door then too. "Let's hope they do before Oliver does."

Oliver snorted out a quick laugh when he saw Qasim approaching. "Tell my sister not to worry. I'm not gonna drive off half-crazed into the night."

Qasim chuckled. "I kind of figured that." He joined Oliver on the steps of the minipatio that faced the east vineyard.

Oliver presented Qasim with one of the three remaining beers sweating on the steps where he'd been sitting since storming out of the house.

"Is Minka okay? I didn't mean to leave the way I did...only...looking at her makes me angry enough to want Will Lloyd dead by my own hand."

"You don't have to explain that to me." Qasim's jaw clenched as he handled the bottle.

"I swear I don't blame her for any of this, Sim. If anyone's to blame, it's me for not making her tell me everything there was to tell about that jackass."

"Neither of you is at fault." Qasim swigged down a bit of the imported brew. "If we're gonna play the blame game, I can take part for not putting Will's ass in jail when *I* had the chance."

Oliver gave into a ripple of abrupt laughter. "We're quite the group of crazies, huh?"

The guys enjoyed their drinks in silence for a while before conversation returned.

"She knows where the fool works and was trying to bring him down on her own," Oliver grimly mused.

"The way he went after her…" Sim shook his head. "I know he's pissed about the way things went down, but this…this was reckless. He's gotta know he's screwed after this."

"What are the odds that your old army buddy is going off the rails?"

"PTSD?" Sim asked. "It's a nasty illness for sure… may not be a bad idea to put more security on Minka until we have Will." He hissed a curse. "It's a damn shame. He was a good soldier and a pretty decent friend, but going after Minka the way he did…that I can't forgive."

"Got to keep an eye on her," Oliver warned. "In spite of what happened, I'm betting she still wants to go after him."

Qasim shook his head. "She blames herself for me not being able to wrap Will up the way I wanted."

"What the hell is she thinking…?"

"Thinking she can do it on her own. She's obsessively independent in case you haven't noticed."

Oliver grinned. "I know the type."

Qasim paused before tipping back more of his beer. "Is that a dig at your sister?"

"Who else?"

"Watch it, Oli. That's my fiancée you're talkin' about."

"You finally asked her?" Oliver's pensive expression mellowed and a grin curved his mouth.

Qasim feigned upset. "Why was everybody so sure I would?"

"Hmph." Oliver shrugged. "It's easier for folks to see things from the outside sometimes."

"So I take it you approve?"

"You know it." Oliver chuckled. "And you know you already got Dad's blessing."

Qasim nodded. "I actually went to see Mr. B before I asked Vectra."

"Does Vecs know that?"

Sim shook his head. "Not sure she'd appreciate it as much as *you* seem to."

Oliver laughed even harder. "Ah...the allure of an independent woman." He sighed as his laughter cooled and then extended a hand to Qasim. "Congrats, man. Are you sure you want to be part of our family after tonight?"

"Hell, yes." Qasim shook Oliver's hand vigorously. "Most people have to pay to see fights that good."

They clinked beer bottles and took long gulps.

Chapter 16

"So when do you think she'll want you to start?" Qasim asked as he wolfed down a mouthful of breakfast potatoes and fluffy eggs.

Minka shook her head while adding a fresh pat of butter to her second biscuit. Vectra and head housekeeper Charlotte Sweeny had settled her in a plush guest room the night before. Minka had slept deeply after the fireworks of the evening.

The smells of a breakfast tray in the room woke her around 10:00 a.m. She was surprised and pleased to have both Qasim and Vectra join her for breakfast. It was a sweet, informal gathering, with Vectra eating where Minka sat near the headboard and Qasim at the foot of the bed.

"Gram wants folks to be aware of the change right

away, but she understands my obligations to Wilder," Minka explained.

"Which means you've got about two weeks." Sim chuckled when Minka pretended to toss her napkin in his direction.

"Better not let Z hear you with that," Minka warned.

Qasim gave a noncommittal shrug. "Miss Z. loves me."

"I guess it was your grandmother who insisted Qasim come aboard as the legal advisor," Vectra noted once her laughter settled.

Minka smiled. "Actually it was my granddad, but Gram wasn't far behind in giving her support. They both fell in love with Sim right away."

Vectra's light eyes went dreamy as she caught her fiancé's gaze across the bed. "I can totally understand that."

Minka looked from Qasim to Vectra. "Guys, I'm sorry about the way dinner turned out. Vectra, you were sweet to invite me."

"Ah." Vectra waved her hand before returning to fork up a few potatoes. "Trust me, we'll have many more dinners leading up to the big day."

"Celebrating the—" Minka's gaze narrowed. "The big day?"

Vectra raised her left hand and wagged her ring finger to show off a stunning chocolate diamond. "I was smart enough to accept," she said.

Minka gasped, quickly setting aside her food tray. Vectra and Qasim set down their plates in anticipation of being hugged. They were gathered in the middle of the bed and in the midst of a three-way embrace when a knock hit the door and Oliver looked inside the room. He smiled at the sight.

"Am I interrupting?" His eyes were locked on Minka.

Minka looked to Vectra. "Does Oliver know?"

Vectra beamed. "Qasim told him last night."

"I just heard about the engagement." Minka sent a shaky smile toward Oliver.

His smile broadened as he looked to the happy couple. "It's the best news I've heard in a while."

The heavy silence that settled then was saved from becoming too ominous when Vectra scooted from the bed, taking her plate with her. "We'll just get out of your hair." She nodded toward Qasim, who followed suit.

"Hey." Oliver caught his sister by the arm when she got close. "I'm sorry for the way I behaved last night."

"Hush." Vectra put a playful slap to the side of his handsome face. "You'll only have to apologize next week when you do something else to piss me off."

Laughter emerged between the siblings as they hugged. Oliver shook hands with Qasim and then took the spot he'd vacated at the foot of the bed.

"I really am sorry about last night," he said to Minka.

She shook her head. "It wasn't your fault."

"The way I left, the things I said before I walked out. Yeah, Mink, that was all on me, and I *am* sorry."

She nodded, watching as Oliver left the bed to retrieve her food tray.

"You eat while I talk," he ordered.

Minka made an effort to do so, but her appetite was gone. She was far more interested in hearing what he had to say.

"I was obviously coming apart at the seams last night." Oliver leaned over to rest his elbows on denim-clad knees. "What that dunce said to you, the fact that he touched you… I honestly believe I would've killed him if I could've gotten my hands on him." He turned to look directly at Minka. "I *would* have killed him if I'd gotten my hands on him."

"That would only make things worse." Minka's voice sounded small.

"I know it's dangerous thinking." Oliver nodded. "It's my anger talking."

"I know about Vectra. She told me about the abuse."

Oliver rubbed at his eyes while a muscle danced viciously along his cheek. "It was a hard time, even harder given the fact that we knew the snake. He was right there the whole time, and we never suspected he was hurting her. When she told me and Dad to stay out of it—" he chuckled "—I think we both went a little crazy."

"Oliver." Minka scooted closer to where he sat. "I didn't think there was anything to tell. I never thought he'd go after me that way, never thought he held *that* much resentment over what happened."

"I know you didn't." Oliver moved closer. "I didn't tell you that because I was fishing for any additional explanations. I only wanted you to know the rest of the story.

"It's not easy to love—watching what my dad went through after my mom passed, watching what Vectra went through. One wrong move by that idiot she was attached to could've been her death sentence. The idea of love and loss terrifies me, Minka. I don't mind admitting that. I'm not proud of it, but I don't mind admitting it."

"I understand." She squeezed his arm.

"Really?" Surprise registered on his handsome, cinnamon-doused features. "Then maybe you could tell me why the fear of loss is becoming a smaller blip on my radar?"

Minka smiled, looking down at her remaining breakfast, which she'd lost complete interest in. "I've heard that love does that."

"Yeah." Oliver nodded, smiled and took her hand. "Yeah, I've heard that somewhere." He gave a tug until they were engaging in a slow, sweet kiss across Minka's breakfast tray.

They broke apart in laughter when the tray hindered how close they wanted to be. Oliver dutifully set it aside, and their kissing resumed. The buttons along the front of her borrowed sleep shirt offered only a minor hindrance.

Minka relished Oliver's touch, which melted away any residual effects from her harrowing experience. He tended to her nipples with infinite care and gentleness until Minka arched beneath him, hungering for more.

The knocking on the door barely registered, but Oliver noticed.

"Are you kidding me?" he muttered.

"Have you guys made up yet?" Vectra's voice drifted in behind the knock.

Minka laughed while Oliver turned his head toward the door.

"We're tryin'!" he yelled.

Zena Moritz Gerald sat across from her granddaughter on an elegant settee embroidered with her initials. Poised, cool, she raised a delicate china cup to her lips and sipped her tea that filled the room with the rich aroma of bergamot.

"And why am I just hearing about this now?"

Minka sighed, shifting her position on the wing chair in the office where she'd joined her grandmother for afternoon tea. She knew honesty was best, and that Zena would sniff out anything less faster than she could blink.

"You're just hearing about it because Sim has placed security guards on me and plans to amp up security at the stockholders event. The security you already have in place will definitely notice the addition of more men."

"Mmm…" Zena continued to sip her tea, knowing that she was heightening anticipation of her response until it reached agonizing proportions.

"Otherwise, you hadn't intended to tell me a thing?" Zena kept her eyes on her teacup while posing the question.

"No." Minka swallowed down a wave of nerves.

Zena at last showed signs of agitation. She set the ornately designed cup on an end table that matched her settee.

"I'm starting to have second thoughts about letting you take the helm, Babylove. Ah, ah…" She raised a hand when Minka piped up to speak. "It doesn't have anything to do with your business savvy, sweetness. It's the fact that you're so careless with your own life. I'll probably have to look for a new successor anyway once you get yourself killed."

Minka cleared her throat, but otherwise remained silent.

"Who else knew about this?" Zena turned to pin her with a look when there was no response.

Minka rolled her eyes. "Mr. Walt and Lorna." She waited for Zena to explode. She frowned curiously when the woman merely smirked and shook her head.

"They wanted you to know, Gram, but I made them promise not to tell."

Zena slowly made her way toward Minka, whose eyes widened in suspicion when the woman patted her head and then dragged a hand through her hair.

"Lord, could you be any more like me?" Zena came round to sit on the arm of the chair. "I commend you for at least taking someone into your confidence."

Minka turned wide eyes up to her grandmother. "I never meant to be deceptive."

"Oh, honey-lump, I know." Zena laughed. "You just didn't want me to worry. So I'll save you from the lecture your grandfather gave me when I tried to handle certain ugliness on *my* own and refused to include him. Don't even try it.

"I know you know the story. Your mother's mother worked for Bry's company back when it was only a hole in the wall. Millicent was there when I came on board.

"I was the high yellow hussy who took Bry from his then fiancée and proceeded to not only marry the man, but to presume I understood how to run his business."

Minka smiled. Of course she knew the story. "Gramp B. was a billionaire because of you."

"Damn right." Zena laughed along with Minka before her expression changed. "I'd do it all again, you know? I'd take all the insults and innuendo…it was all worth it for that glorious time I had with your granddad. The only thing I'd do differently would be to perhaps let go of some of that independence. It's a wonderful thing, but it can sometimes be a person's worst enemy.

Especially if it prevents us from reaching out for help from those who love us."

Minka toyed with the fringe cuff of Zena's burgundy lounge dress and absorbed the advice.

"Your grandfather made me see that I didn't have to handle all that stuff that went down in the early days on my own. I'm glad you sought Walt's and Lorna's help, Babylove, but you're about to be brought out of the shadows. Your life is about to change." She patted Minka's cheek. "I'd like to see you with a truly special someone who can support you through the coming years."

Minka sent her grandmother a cunning smile. "I know you suspect there's something between me and Oliver Bauer."

Zena looked delighted. "He is a delicious-looking thing, isn't he? Rose and Oscar put together a very fine specimen. Very fine." Some of her delight melded into concern. "But I hear he's quite the ladies' man."

"He says he loves me. His sister says it's not a word he's prone to use, not even with family."

"And I suppose she would know." Zena fiddled with the upturned collar of Minka's blazer dress. "I guess the important thing though is what *you* think about it."

Minka touched her fingers to her lips to hide her smile. "I believe him," she said.

Zena looked pleased. "And how do you feel about him?"

"I love him, Gram."

Zena appeared doubly pleased. She clapped once and dropped a kiss to the top of Minka's head. "So I guess the next logical question is whether I should turn tonight's event into an engagement party."

Laughing, Minka eased her arms about her grand-mother's trim waist and hugged her.

Zena planted a second kiss to Minka's head. "Be happy," she whispered.

The annual BGI shareholders' meeting was always a study in excess. Zena Gerald thought it gave the hold-ers confidence in the company's security. As if that was ever in question, given BGI's consistently stellar per-formance in the market.

At any rate, Zena made it her mission to go all out for the event. A diverse array of caterers was on hand to provide dishes for a variety of buffets. Live perform-ers brought musical entertainment from a selection of genres.

The Gerald mansion was a vast gold-lit portrayal of elegance. Guests made their way inside on the royal blue carpet that ran the length of the wide drive. The stream of blue velvet disappeared inside the expansive foyer that shimmered from the effects of the electric candlelight and chandeliers.

Minka had given Oliver the particulars of the event and he seemed eager to attend. She observed the gath-ering from her perch at the foyer stairway—a row of five steps on either side of the space that arched up and led to the great room.

She had spent the previous night and day with her grandmother, but Oliver had promised to meet her here. She had yet to spot him. In an attempt to keep her mind off his absence, Minka made her rounds about the room. Zena had yet to make her grand announcement, but it was obvious from the manner of the guests that the news was already well known.

Dressed in a curvy gown the color of merlot, with side splits that offered seductive glimpses of calf and thigh, Minka made several successful turns about the room. She discovered that the experience wasn't as harrowing as she'd expected it would be. Feeling accomplished, she took a flute of champagne from a passing server and decided to grab a bit of fresh air on the empty terrace.

"I wasn't sure if I was arriving at the Gerald mansion or Fort Knox when I got here."

Minka turned in the direction of the voice and smiled at Calvin Spring. They walked out to the terrace together. "My grandmother would enjoy that comparison."

Spring laughed. "It's quite the gathering, that's for sure." He looked behind them into the house, which teemed with guests. "I can understand the need for the extra security."

Minka gave a weak smile.

"I'm afraid the extra security is my fault because of Will's attack the other night." Spring sighed, looking as though he'd lost his taste for the gin in the tumbler he held. "Guess I should look into some extra security myself. We told the police he's been out sick for several days. I still don't understand why he would attack *you*?"

Minka's curiosity had heightened the longer Spring talked. "He holds me responsible for losing his job at Wilder. Remember I told you about his time there when we spoke over the phone?"

"Well the folks I've got shadowing him won't miss a thing if he gives them something to sniff out."

"Calvin." Minka set her glass on a ledge. "Be careful. I don't want anyone else getting hurt over this."

Calvin stepped in to squeeze Minka's elbow. "Don't worry, the creep won't even know my folks are looking over his shoulder."

"You wanna bet on that, boss?"

Minka and Spring turned at once, both jolted by the sight of Will Lloyd, emerging from behind a stone pillar. He was carrying a gleaming knife.

Calvin reached for Minka and tugged her behind him.

"What a gentleman," Will sneered. "Or maybe it's just about protecting the hand that feeds you." His glare moved to Minka. "I stopped in to check things out at the office today, unnoticed, of course. Imagine my surprise when I discovered I knew a real-life billionaire. All that time posing as one of us normal folks. Did you get off on seeing how the other half lives, Ms. Gerald?"

Minka scanned the terrace, but everyone was still inside. *Figures*, she groaned inwardly.

"Am I boring you, princess?" He moved closer to Calvin Spring, his gaze never leaving Minka's face. "Let's see if we can do something to keep the princess interested, boss." He landed a vicious kick to Spring's midsection and quickly grabbed Minka while Spring doubled over from the impact of the blow.

Minka's scream was muffled by Will's hand clamping down hard over her mouth. "Don't worry, princess, your shining knight will be joining us." Jerking Minka along, Will put another punishing kick to Spring's ankle and smirked when the man groaned. "On your feet, boss. This is on you, Minka," he sneered while Spring made an effort to stand. "If you had just kept your nose out of my business—"

"It was Qasim's business, not yours." Minka tried to

wrench free of Will's hold on her arm. "Did you even give the slightest damn that you were stealing from kids? *Kids*, Will? As a soldier, didn't that bother you?"

"Shut your mouth." Will gave her another punishing tug.

Spring was finally on his feet and tottering toward Will and Minka. Will showed his displeasure of Spring's dragging movements and jabbed the man's spine with the tip of the knife. Minka and Spring screamed at once, but the knife jab drew no blood.

"Damn you, Will." Minka renewed her struggles, somehow holding on to her courage. "You were a soldier, weren't you? How can you threaten the lives of people you went to war to protect?!" She knew she was taking an awful risk in trying to reason with him, but was gambling on the fact that a shred of the honorable soldier was still somewhere to be found.

"What the hell do you know about being a soldier? You think that life is a cakewalk? Do you?!"

Minka gasped, her courage oozing away. Spring stepped forward. "Will, man—"

"Back! You get the hell back!" Will showed his boss the grisly weapon. "You don't know what the hell we went through over there. Nightmare isn't even the word for it. As bad as it was though, I'd take it all again for the world of crap I got handed to me over here."

"Not everyone's story is the same as yours, Will." Minka felt some of her bravery returning. "Things aren't perfect, but they have changed."

"That's what people like you want to believe." Will held Minka flush against his chest while glaring at Spring. "You big shots sittin' on your high hills, closed up behind your gilded doors. Nothing touches you, nothing matters until someone like me goes for a piece of the pie."

"That pie wasn't yours, Will," Minka gritted out. "You weren't entitled to a slice."

Will's smile was purely sinister. "Do we really want to talk about slices, Ms. Gerald?" He brought the knife in closer to Minka's cheek.

"Lloyd, don't!" Spring lunged forward, hands outstretched.

Will retaliated by hurtling the knife into Spring's arm. Spring crumpled while Will laughed over his agony. He wrenched Minka along as he went to retrieve the weapon. Will's focus was on reclaiming his knife. Minka said a swift prayer, squeezed her eyes shut and rammed her elbow high between his ribs. She heard his stunned grunt as his hand loosened from her arm. She wasted no time breaking into a run.

Minka stumbled a bit in her pumps but remained upright and ran screaming toward the party.

Will quickly recovered from the blow. Turning his attention back to Spring, he grabbed the knife, checked his grip on the handle and prepared to launch it at Minka's departing figure.

Minka heard a thud and risked a look over her shoulder. She stumbled to a stop. Stunned, she saw Oliver standing over Will's body. Will was hunched on all fours, drawing in ragged breaths as a heavy stream of blood oozed from his nose and upper lip.

Oliver was moving in to deliver more blows, but he froze at the sound of Minka's voice saying his name. The fierce haze seemed to lift from his brain, and he stepped over Will. He drew Minka into a crushing hug as swarms of security arrived on the terrace to take Will into custody.

Minka could feel Oliver trembling as he held her. "I'm okay," she soothed.

Oliver needed more proof, apparently. He lifted Minka off her feet, looked her over head to toe and then buried his handsome face into the side of her neck. For long moments, he breathed her in and squeezed her in an ever tightening embrace.

Guards helped Spring to his feet. Guests who had gotten wind of the incident had congregated at the French doors that bordered the terrace.

Minka relaxed into Oliver's arms.

CG Spring's terrified call rang out seconds after Will overpowered the guard who had moved in the closest. Will relieved the man of his weapon in one swift, expert move, indicative of his military training.

Despite the fact that he was outgunned, Will was determined not to go down without a fight. He blindly aimed the gun, but received a round to his calf before he could fire. A second shot hit his shoulder. Losing his footing, Will stumbled back against the terrace's stone railing.

Minka's scream mingled with those of other guests as Will Lloyd faltered back off the terrace edge and disappeared from sight.

"Déjà vu."

Minka managed a wavery smile when Oliver's voice rumbled into her ear where she rested against his chest. All she wanted was to shield her gaze from all the concerned stares and the hustle of bodies as people worked to make sense of the night's events.

Qasim and Vectra walked into the small den where Zena had whisked Oliver and Minka off to. Her dark eyes widened expectantly and locked with Qasim's.

"How's Will?" she asked.

"The fall broke his leg in three places." Grimness cast an even darker element to Qasim's features. "That won't be a happy accompaniment to the gunshot wound in his other leg. And that shoulder of his is gonna need some TLC for the foreseeable future."

"Will he go to jail after this?" Vectra asked.

"He'll go to jail *during* this," Qasim confirmed. "He'll be in custody around the clock during his recovery."

"Is he sick, Qasim?" Minka's voice was small.

Qasim's grim expression intensified. He understood what Minka was really asking. "I'm no doctor, and it sours something inside me to think the bastard could get away with being a jealous, self-centered snake. But I wouldn't be surprised if he were given a diagnosis of post-traumatic stress disorder."

Oliver expelled a curse. "Either way I think we can safely expect him to be institutionalized for the foreseeable future, in either a hospital or a prison."

"He should get help if he needs it," Minka said, burrowing deeper into Oliver's chest.

Smiling, Oliver squeezed her closer. "Will you ever stop looking out for people?"

"This wasn't your fault, Mink," Qasim said.

"I know." She nodded. "But he won't be any use to himself or anyone else if he doesn't get the help he needs. He fought for his country—he deserves at least that much and definitely more."

"And you wonder why I love you." Oliver leaned close to kiss her.

Vectra caught Qasim's eye, and they left the couple alone.

"Mmm…I'm sooo ready to spend the night in my own bed…" Minka sighed the words after a restful night's sleep.

Seconds later, she discovered two things: she wasn't alone, and what she had snuggled her head into wasn't a pillow. She looked up, smiling into Oliver's gorgeous face.

"I definitely agree with you," he said drowsily. "Do you know how hard it was for me to be on my best behavior in your grandmother's house?"

Minka laughed. "I don't think we would've shocked her."

"I'm not risking it." Oliver drew a hand through his hair and shook his head against the pillow. "I'm doin' my damndest to get myself accepted as the woman's grandson-in-law."

Minka blinked, her eyes wide.

"Did I say something?" Oliver knew full well he'd stunned her speechless.

"I…can be hard to handle," was all she managed.

"I like that." Oliver set his hand beneath his head on the pillow and shrugged. "Means I don't have to worry that I'm not being gentle enough."

"Oliver." Minka pushed up, bracing her weight to her elbows as she looked down at him. "What you said about me having to look out for other people… my grandmother said I'm just like her and that she…

the way she is…was sometimes a big challenge for my granddad."

"Mmm…and yet they had a long, satisfying marriage…"

"They did…" Minka considered the truth while toying with a heavy curl dangling close to her eye. "But we're out the gate with some pretty heavy stuff."

"Damn right, and I haven't even started browsing for rings yet."

"Be serious."

Oliver's playful expression sharpened at once. "Don't think for a minute that I'm not." His hand disappeared in her curls, and he snagged a hoard of them. "I know what I want. You're it—good, bad and beautiful. I love you."

"I love you too," she said as he pulled her astride his lap. He began to fondle a plump breast beneath the T-shirt she'd pulled from the stash of lounge attire she kept in her guest room.

He leaned in for a heavy kiss, and Minka could scarcely find the energy to meet the thorough thrusts and rotations of his tongue. She was too enthralled by the sensation roused by his seeking hands.

Minka eased her hips to make room for his fingers skimming the silky folds of her sex, already growing slick with her need. Her moan reverberated in the room.

"Hush up, will you?" Oliver commanded in a whisper.

"But my bedroom is in its own private wing."

"Can't take any chances, remember?"

Their kiss resumed, full-blown and lusty. Minka rode Oliver's exploring fingers as they took her with a merciless enthusiasm. She was intermittently bucking her hips to absorb the sensual ripples of the touch and arching her chest to indulge in the erotic assault on her nipples.

"Oliver?" She felt him leave the bed. "Where...?" was all she could muster when he took her with him.

"Back to bed, after I do this."

Minka felt the bedroom door behind her back, and, moments later, the turn of the lock touched her ears. She released the giggle that tickled her throat. "Are things about to get *that* shocking?"

"You've got no idea," Oliver said with a sly wink as he headed back to bed with his lovely, laughing woman.

* * * * *

This summer is going to be hot, hot, hot
with a new miniseries
from fan-favorite authors!

YAHRAH ST. JOHN
LISA MARIE PERRY
PAMELA YAYE

HEAT WAVE
OF DESIRE

Available June 2015

HOT SUMMER
NIGHTS

Available July 2015

HEAT OF
PASSION

Available August 2015

California Desert Dreams

Their affair is this
exclusive resort's
best-kept secret

HEAT *of* PASSION

PAMELA YAYE

Robyn Henderson, Belleza Resort's head event planner, is throwing
the charity event of the season. But when a series of bizarre incidents
hit, evidence points to LA restaurateur Sean Parker, Robyn's secret
crush—and her best friend's brother. As Sean fights to clear his name,
he must decide where his future lies. But can he also convince Robyn
to trust in their love?

California Desert Dreams

"A compelling page-turner from start to finish."
—*RT Book Reviews* on *SEDUCED BY MR. RIGHT*

HARLEQUIN®
www.Harlequin.com

Available August 2015!

KPPY4130815

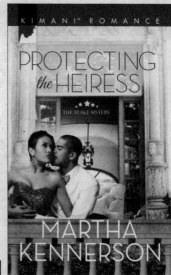

REQUEST YOUR FREE BOOKS!

2 FREE NOVELS
PLUS 2 FREE GIFTS!

KIMANI
ROMANCE
TM

Love's ultimate destination!

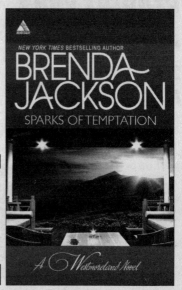

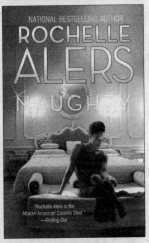

H™ BESTSELLING AUTHOR COLLECTION

CLASSIC ROMANCES IN COLLECTIBLE VOLUMES

New York Times **Bestselling Author**

BRENDA JACKSON

Sometimes a knight in shining armor wears a cowboy hat

Seven years ago, as a young cop, Darius Franklin saved a vulnerable woman from a violent situation. They shared one night of pure passion before she walked away. Now Darius is a wealthy rancher and security contractor working at a women's shelter. And he's shocked to meet the new social worker: Summer Martindale, a beautiful damsel no longer in distress.

ONE NIGHT WITH THE WEALTHY RANCHER

"Brenda Jackson writes romance that sizzles and characters you fall in love with." —*New York Times* bestselling author Lori Foster

Available August 2015 wherever books are sold!